3013: CLAIMED

3013: THE SERIES

Laurie Roma

The 3013 Series

3013: MATED by Laurie Roma
3013: RENEGADE by Susan Hayes
3013: CLAIMED by Laurie Roma
3013: STOWAWAY by Susan Hayes

3013: CLAIMED

As one of Earth's greatest leaders, Commander Jax Spartan lives his life by a strict code. Dedicated and alpha to the core, he is the epitome of what every Elite soldier aspires to be. Second-in-command Sullivan Archer rules by his best friend's side, and together they form an unstoppable force that few are foolish enough to challenge. Jax and Archer have always known they'd share their chosen, but their hearts have already been claimed by the woman they've vowed will belong to them.

Alliance scientist Serra Lysander is a genius who has kept the planet safe with her inventions. She's lived a sheltered life, separated from society by her brilliant mind and her overprotective mother. The only time Serra has truly ever felt accepted is with the two men that will cost her everything…

When danger leads Serra straight into the arms of Jax and Archer, they will do anything to keep her safe, even claiming her despite the fact she is off limits. With the future of the Alliance on the line, will their love and dedication be enough to save them, or will they be too late to stop the growing threat from destroying them all?

An Erotic Romance Novel.

3013: CLAIMED by Laurie Roma
First Print Publication: June 2014
Print Edition

Cover design by Sloan Winters
Editing by S.L. Whitcomb

Copyright © 2014 by Laurie Roma

DEDICATION

To all the readers and fans of the 3013 Series,

Thank you for embracing the 3013 world, and allowing us to entertain you. We are so pleased to share our world with you, if only for a little while. Until the next book…

Prologue

The year is 3013.

Earth barely survived the Alien Wars that have ravaged the planet, and an unknown virus had nearly wiped out the entire population. On the brink of extinction, humans struggle to rebuild their civilization, although nothing would ever bring back what once was.

Enforcing martial law, a new age of mankind is born, where warriors rule and women are the ultimate prize. Only the elite earn breeding rights and are granted leave to claim a woman in pairs. Men dream of the day that they will be able to claim a woman to love, but for those chosen being claimed means the end of their freedom and a beginning to a lifelong bond with two strangers. The warriors may have the choice, but the battle for their woman's heart has only begun…

Chapter One

"She's even more beautiful than I remember."

Commander Jax Spartan didn't turn as his best friend and second-in-command, Sullivan Archer, spoke upon entering the dark viewing room. Jax silently agreed, but didn't feel the need to say anything in response.

There was no need.

Jax's body was rigid with tension as he stared through the double-sided mirror at the woman seated in the adjacent interrogation room. The room was dark, and had been made so with the purpose of unnerving a suspect. The walls were made of a dark-gray, foam-like substance to deter someone from hurting themselves by slamming against it. God knew that some of the suspects they'd interrogated would have rather killed themselves then face Alliance law, but they weren't given that option. There were three spotlights shining down from the ceiling, all pointed toward the chair designated for the suspect.

The woman currently highlighted under the glaring lights didn't belong in there.

Serra Lysander's beautiful face was paler than usual against the austere backdrop of the room. Her dark-brown hair was ruthlessly pulled back into a chignon, leaving her heart-shaped face clear to Jax's view. He knew that once that thick mass of hair was let loose, it would cascade over her shoulders in a sleek waterfall of dark silk. His hands fisted at his sides and his fucking heart actually ached seeing the stark terror mixed with confusion in her pale-green eyes.

Serra was the most beautiful woman they'd ever seen, and both he and Archer knew it.

In contrast to the interrogation chamber, the viewing room had been decorated with comfort in mind. The walls were painted a dark gold color, and there were several chairs and a couch at the far side of the room all made of a rich, brown leather that was both comfortable and stylish. Off to the side of the room was a standard food console that could replicate drinks and basic fare upon command. It felt fucking wrong to be surrounded by such a lavish setting when Serra was left in shadows.

Jax saw Archer standing next to him out of the corner of his eye, and knew that his friend had taken up a similar stance. Both of them were battle ready. Rage swept through Jax as he watched Regent Marie Wyland-Ross and High Commander Roman Newgate talking to Serra on the other side of the glass.

No, not talking.

Interrogating.

Unlike Jax and Archer, who both wore the standard uniform of a steel-gray jacket with off-center zipper, black sleeves and regulation black pants and boots, Regent Wyland-Ross wore the black uniform with red sleeves that designated her Regent status, while High Commander Newgate wore the black uniform with white sleeves that signified his position with high command. Both of them looked severe compared to Serra, who was dressed in light grey pants and a pretty lilac colored blouse that seemed to make her innocent green eyes look even brighter.

She didn't belong there, Jax thought again, and it infuriated him that he hadn't known she had been taken into custody before he could stop it. Oh, he was damn sure they were being gentle with her. Jax had made it clear before this farce began that he would have their asses if they treated her with anything less than respect while they questioned her.

There weren't too many men on planet that would ever dare threaten a regent or high commander, but Jax wasn't just any man. He was a commander under the rule of the United Federation Command Alliance and was in charge of the Capital, Earth's largest and most prosperous city. Although most commanders reported to high command, Jax had been given leave to report directly to the Alliance Council of Regents. The Regents were made up of retired military commanders from all of the territories, and acted as the governing body of the Alliance. Jax held the entire Council in high regard, but there was no one he wouldn't challenge to keep Serra safe.

"The two of you shouldn't be in here."

Jax's body stiffened even more as he heard the voice behind him, and the fury he felt threatened to break free. Slowly turning his head, he focused his eyes on the man who had spoken, like a predator would his prey. "If she's here then so are we, but I've had enough. This ends now."

Archer grunted in agreement as Jax finally turned away from the viewing window. He'd seen enough. Now it was time to end whatever game the regents were playing. He braced his feet apart and crossed his arms over his massive chest. At six-foot-seven he knew he was a large, intimidating man, but the two male regents glaring at him were not impressed.

Like all elite soldiers in the Alliance, he'd been genetically enhanced. The enhancements gave males additional muscle mass, making them larger and more adept at fighting. At the age of ten, all children under Alliance rule were tested. For the girls it was to determine if they were to receive the scroll tattoo near their eye, marking them as one of the rare fertile females, and for the boys it was to determine if they would be taken for military service.

Only the strongest and brightest males were chosen for the biological enhancements to become elite soldiers. The elites were bigger and stronger than normal humans, with increased reflexes and heightened senses. These enhancements were encoded into their genes, and would be passed onto their children.

Their enhanced genetics were the future of the human race.

When Jax had undergone the enhancements, he had been given an extra bonus—or curse— depending how one looked at it. He'd gotten the increased strength that all elites received, only he'd developed...more. The enhancement process tended to amplify attributes individuals already possessed. Jax had already been a natural leader, but he'd also been born with character traits that made him more alpha than most. With the genetic enhancements, those traits were increased to the point that Jax had to keep a tight leash on his dominant nature and focus on reining in his need to control everything around him. At times he felt more animal than man, especially when he was really angry.

And this was definitely one of those moments…

Sullivan Archer was the luckier of the two. With the elite enhancements, Archer's observation skills had been heightened to an incredible degree. He could tell if someone was lying just from watching the pulse on their neck, and there was little he couldn't see with the barest glance around a room. As the quieter one of the pair, it gave Archer the added advantage of standing back while most people reacted to Jax, giving him time to assess a situation before both of them struck out with their combined force.

No one stood a chance against them.

And now it was time to settle this before both of them lost control of their tempers.

Regent Everett Marks sighed as he eyed both Jax and Archer warily. "You know there is a need to question Ms. Lysander. This matter is too important to just let her walk away. When I received word about the potential sale of the new stealth technology Ms. Lysander has been working on, I didn't want to believe it either. She's been instrumental in protecting Earth and the Alliance. Why, her creation of the new shield that guards Earth and all of our sub-stations has saved countless of lives. But we have to consider how many unsanctioned sales of that shield tech have been discovered in the last year. It's extremely troubling."

"Serra would never sell any technology to outsiders, sanctioned or unsanctioned. She knows the ramifications too well to do that," Archer snapped, his control fraying at the edges. "Besides, she has never had anything to do with sales of any of her tech. She hands everything she does over to the Alliance. If there is a problem then that's where we should be looking. The other people working on this project."

"We are, but she isn't that girl you once knew. Not anymore," the other regent said softly.

Jax held up his hand for silence, his fury radiating off him in waves. "We know her. She didn't do this."

"You can't be sure of that."

"I am."

"By God, are you stubborn!"

"I wonder where I came by that trait…father." Jax eyed Regent Spartan with a hint of amusement, despite his anger.

Regent Ian Spartan glared at his son. "Don't you start with me. As I said before, you two shouldn't even be here. You may have known Serra Lysander when you were young, but you don't know her any longer. Things change."

Jax was done arguing about this.

No one knew the extent of Jax and Archer's history with Serra. They had made sure of it. The truth was that they knew Serra better than any other person on the planet, or off. She had only been twelve years old when they had met her back when both he and Archer were teens, barely more than children themselves. He and Archer had already developed a kick-ass reputation in the Academy when Serra had been moved into training with the older teens…and nothing had ever been the same.

For any of them.

Elite soldiers were trained to be the best, in every way, and that training was rigorous in many disciplines. Not only were they regularly tested for physical strength and endurance, they were all tested in a multitude of mental assessments that helped place them for service when they were older. Aptitude for certain subjects allowed each soldier to focus on what department or service they were best suited for, giving them direction and purpose.

From the moment Jax had been tested, he knew that he was destined for command. All three of his parents had strong leadership qualities. Jax's natural father, Ian Spartan, had risen through the ranks to the lofty position of regent, becoming one of the youngest members on the ruling council. His other father, Jack Rollins, had retired from service when they had claimed Jax's mother. It was an old family joke that it was a full-time position keeping their chosen out of trouble, and Jack was more than happy to take on that duty.

Jax's mother, Donna Spartan-Rollins, had started a fashion empire called Starlight Designs, catering to some of the wealthiest members of the Alliance before she had been claimed. As a woman with a good heart, she used her position of power to give back through numerous charities, but she also made it her personal mission to look out for the young children in the Academy whenever she could.

Unlike other mothers within the Alliance who practically handed their children over once they entered the training facilities, Donna refused to stop looking out for Jax or his siblings once they turned ten. As the oldest of four children, Jax considered himself the test case. He often told his younger brothers and sister that their parents had worked out most of their neurosis by the time Jax had graduated from the Academy.

Back when Jax was young, his parents had changed the conditions of the training facilities in the Capital. Ian and Jack had been used to the barren environment of the Academy, but Donna had been horrified when she'd gone to visit. She would not rest until the facility looked more like a school than a military barracks. Jax's fathers had tried to protest, but there was nothing they wouldn't do for their chosen, and Donna was a frightening force to be reckoned with when she wanted something.

Outraged that some of the other parents had abandoned their own children, Donna had opened the Spartan-Rollins home to Jax's friends, and to anyone who had nowhere else to go when they were given leave from the training facility. Learning from all three of his parents, Jax had become a champion of those who had no one to fight for them.

Sullivan Archer had been one of those children.

16

Left on the doorstep of one of the Alliance outposts in the outskirts of the badlands, Archer had started his life as an orphan. He'd never known who his mother or father were, and they obviously hadn't cared about him enough to raise him themselves. He was just another nameless child, another mouth to feed out in a place where resources were scarce.

Fortunately, he had been taken in by a pair of elite soldiers who had fallen in love with an infertile woman who ran an orphanage located in the outpost. The female children were always taken in by families, but the boys…they were left to fend for themselves until they became old enough to be tested. All of the elites on that particular base had taken turns helping raise the children. They were luckier than other innocents that had been thrown away, but it still didn't mean they had a place where they truly belonged.

After Archer turned ten and went through testing, he had been sent to the Capital and enrolled in the Academy. Far from his foster family, he had been scared and alone…until he met Jax. From the moment they had started training together, the two of them had become fast friends. Where Jax had black hair, steel-gray eyes and a quick temper, Archer was his opposite, with burnished gold hair, light-brown eyes and a wicked sense of humor. They were the dark and the light, but they had a similar mindset. They balanced each other and grew stronger together.

Working with Jax, Archer had finally found his place.

Several years later, Archer had been the first to recognize a fellow lost soul in Serra. Jax had been concerned when they had seen the frightened young girl thrown in among them, but it quickly became clear why the transfer had been made. He and Archer had made an unspoken vow to watch out for her in order to make sure she didn't get lost in the sea of recruits.

Before Serra was given the enhancements, she had already shown promise of being extremely intelligent, but after, she surpassed even genius level. She had been lost, terrified by her new surroundings. Her advanced mental capabilities had ensured that she would never fit into normal society, and something in her somber pale-green eyes had touched Jax and Archer. Serra had been almost resigned to the fact that the older recruits resented her for being smarter than them, and her gifts marked her as an oddity who could never fit in.

From the moment they'd met Serra, Jax and Archer had felt an overwhelming urge to protect the little girl with sad eyes too big for her small face. They had quickly ensured that the other recruits knew that anyone messing with her would have to deal with them.

No one wanted to face the wrath of Jax…even back then.

While they were in the Academy, Jax and Archer had taken many recruits under their protection, but there was something special about Serra. Over the two years they had watched over her, she had blossomed out of her shell, but only around them. Whenever she needed comfort, she would run to Archer to wipe away her tears, but she'd always run to Jax to fight her demons. If she were ever scared or worried about anything, Jax was the first person she sought out. His friends used to tease him about his little shadow, but one hard look from him would shut them up.

When they'd graduated from the Academy and had been sent off on their first official assignment on Alpha Station: X1, it had been difficult to say goodbye to Serra. Because of her age, she'd been kept in the training facility. While they were away, the trainers had chosen to have experts in a variety of fields of science and engineering come to the Academy to tutor Serra privately, but losing her two closest friends had destroyed the fragile cocoon of safety she'd felt when they were around.

Jax and Archer had tried to keep in touch with her, but it was difficult to do when they were always working. It wasn't until two years later, when they were able to get reassigned back on Earth, that they came face-to-face with a sixteen year old Serra. Seeing her again had taken their breath away, and that was when those simple protective feelings changed to something more.

Something deeper and harder to explain.

Serra had turned into a beauty while they had been stationed off planet. At sixteen, she had lost the softness that came with youth, and there was a new confidence in her eyes that hadn't been there before. Jax and Archer had only to share a look to know they were in complete accord. They knew that the little girl they had adored with veiled amusement and affection would be the woman they'd one day claim as their chosen.

Unfortunately, they weren't aware their reactions to her were being observed until it was too late. Tania Lysander-Dobbs, Serra's overprotective mother, had taken note of Jax and Archer's interest in her daughter, and had been alarmed by their attention. It wasn't long after their reunion when Tania had pulled Serra out of the Academy and entered her into an internship program off planet.

That had been almost eight years ago.

Jax and Archer had watched with pride as she'd become one of the brightest minds the Alliance ever had working for them, and they had wanted her. Serra's development of the shield that protected Earth and all of the Alliance bases throughout space kept her traveling. During the years that had passed, Jax and Archer's contact with Serra had been reduced to random letters they received from her. They always responded, but she kept their correspondence infrequent, driving them crazy with her resistance to come home. She had an important position, and they knew that, but it didn't mean they'd been happy about it.

Back before she had turned eighteen, Serra had been granted special status due to her contributions to the Alliance when she had signed on as an official inventor. Her new status allowed her to choose her own bonding partners, warning any overzealous elites that there were extreme consequences if she was claimed against her will. It had soothed Jax and Archer's anger when she made it clear she wasn't interested in any other men during her travels.

Still, they'd kept track of Serra wherever she went, watching out for her however they could. She had been appointed three sets of guards who rotated the duty of keeping her safe, and all six men having been warned that if they tried to touch her it would mean their death. Jax hadn't fucked around when he'd made that statement to each of the guards, and he had let them see the truth in his eyes.

Archer had been more subtle with his protection of Serra. Perhaps it had been a little over-the-top, but he had placed a tracker in a small heart necklace made of *xithradite* he'd given her before she had left all those years ago. *Xithradite* was a precious metal found on the Helios planet that shimmered and constantly changed colors, which made it perfect for jewelry. The necklace was beautiful, but it also allowed them to know where she was, in case she ever needed them. Archer had once told Jax that he would delete the program if she ever chose a bonding pair instead of coming back to them, but she never had, so the link remained active.

They knew in their hearts that she was meant for them. She knew it too, but something held her back—something they didn't understand. They had been willing to let her work up her nerve to come to them. Over the last few years they had seen her briefly, and the hunger for her had been growing into a gnawing ache that needed to be sated. Now the time had come and they wouldn't wait any longer.

They had a past, but more important…they had a future.

Jax's patience was at an end and he turned away from the two regents, heading to the door of the viewing room. He had to force himself not to snarl as his father reached out to grip his arm, stopping him before he could open the door. He didn't pull away because the hold was gentle, and he respected his father too much to dishonor him by doing so.

"Jax, this is too important to just let go. We may not have any evidence that she was the one who sold the shield tech, but we cannot let this new stealth technology get into the hands of our enemies."

"She isn't behind this. Where are her guards? I want them questioned."

Regent Ian Spartan released his hold on Jax and huffed out an impatient breath. "Already done. They were also taken into custody when they landed. Two members of the SI Division are with Officers Meyers and Rhine now."

"I've called in my own interrogators from SI. Hold them until my men can interrogate them," Jax ordered. He knew that all the officers of the SI Division were capable, but his friends were the best, and he and Archer would only trust them with Serra.

As soon as Jax had discovered that Serra had been taken into custody, he had made the call to the Capital's Director of the Security and Interrogation Division, Dominic Stryker. Dom was known as a bad-ass that could make a suspect spill his guts with just one hard look of his piercing black eyes. He also had the added advantage of working with Arik V'Dir, one of the few members of the D'Aire alien race that had decided to make Earth his home.

In the year 2960 a new alien race came to Earth called the Zyphir. They'd been a colony race of insect-like creatures that stood on two feet. What they came for was total annihilation of the human race, after which they'd planned to take over Earth and deplete the world of all resources until moving on to the next planet that suited their needs. A three year war ensued, during which a large portions of Earth were destroyed. Not just by battle, but by an unknown virus the Zyphir carried that nearly wiped out the entire population. Without the aid of the Arcadians, Krytos and the D'Aire alien races, Earth would have been nothing but a memory.

Regent Spartan's eyes narrowed. "Who have you called in?"

"Director Stryker and Ambassador V'Dir."

With a satisfied nod, Regent Spartan said, "They are the best. If she's innocent, they'll clear her. The information we have is that the sale for the new stealth technology is set to be held on New Vega in a few weeks. Serra Lysander is booked on a private shuttle for New

Vega before the deadline. That is highly suspicious. Even you have to admit that."

"And why is she back on Earth now?" Regent Marks asked. "She hardly ever comes back on planet, so why has she decided to check out the drones we're testing the stealth tech on? We aren't set to add it to the fleet for another three months, so why is she here now? She arrived here in the Capital. If she is here to examine her creation, why didn't she arrive in Light City where the testing site is? We need to know what the hell she is trying to hide!"

Jax stared at the regents, knowing the older men saw the hard edge that gleamed from his own eyes. "Archer," he snapped.

Knowing what Jax was asking for, Archer stepped forward. "Serra Lysander comes back to Earth every year for a two week period this time a year so she can attend the Freedom Day Gala. She'd never fly into Light City unless she has to, because that is where her fathers are stationed. Since they're more interested in spending their free time with their mistress instead of seeing their daughter, Serra doesn't bother with them. Tania Lysander-Dobbs is sure to stay clear of Earth if Serra is going to be anywhere near her fathers."

"Why would Serra have handed the technology over to the Alliance if she just wanted to sell it?" Jax asked. "If you've looked at her accounts, you know she doesn't care about credits. She hardly spends anything, and has more than she could spend in a lifetime anyways. All her time is focused on work."

"Still, that doesn't explain about the timing of the sale," Regent Marks argued.

Jax turned to glare at the regent. "It's not her, and you're wasting time thinking it is."

Regent Spartan sighed. "Jax, we are doing what we have to in order to protect the Alliance. Hell, to protect Earth. This new stealth program Serra has created far surpasses everything we have to date. Christ, even our systems can't pick it up on scans. Can you imagine what would happen if one of our enemies had that tech? They could get within range to destroy our shields before we even knew they were there. There is too much at stake for us to simply let her go because you believe her."

"Our people are working on a system to detect the stealth mode, but they've hit a wall and can't figure out how to do it." The irritation in Regent Mark's voice was clear. "We have to figure out who is selling our tech and track the buyer so we can shut it down from that end. We need information, and that woman is the key!"

The grin that crossed Archer's face was anything but amused. His amber eyes had a dangerous gleam to them that warned everyone in the room that he wasn't a man to cross. "We'll figure out who is behind this. Believe me." He jerked his head toward the door. "Jax."

Jax nodded then pulled the door open, striding out into the hallway. The two regents scurried out of the room after them, their protests falling on deaf ears. Jax simply glared at the soldier standing guard in front of the closed door to the interrogation room and watched with satisfaction as the poor man shifted to the side with a hunch of his shoulders as if trying to escape notice.

"Jax! Stop ignoring me. You can't go in there," his father growled.

"Watch me."

"Damn it, have some sense! You have no authority in this!"

"Oh, but I will. Anything that has to do with Serra is our business, and therefore gives us the authority to act on her behalf." Jax's smile was feral. "She belongs to us. Consider her claimed."

Chapter Two

Terror was a living, breathing entity inside of Serra.

Since she was young, she'd always had an issue with panic attacks whenever she felt stressed or anxious. Over the years, she'd learned how to stave them off a little better, but right now all of the training she had instilled in herself had disappeared like a puff of smoke.

Treason.

Just the word alone sent icy shivers of fear tingling down her spine. Seeing the watchful way Regent Wyland-Ross and High Commander Newgate studied her from across the table had anxiety spiking through her system like a turbo-booster. They wanted answers she couldn't give. Wanted explanations to things she didn't know what to say in response to, because she simply didn't know.

Her throat felt like the deserts of the badlands, and she tried to hide the shaking of her hands by gripping them together tight. She wanted to explain that the way High Commander Newgate was glaring at her was making it more difficult for her to speak, but she couldn't. The ramifications to whatever response she gave were just too crucial.

If she said something wrong it could cost her everything...even her life.

She was a scientist for the Alliance, an inventor who created technology that helped protect the people of Earth, its allies and throughout space on stations and ships that traveled the galaxy. She had dedicated her life to keeping people safe. Why in god's name would anyone think she had betrayed everything she believed in? And for what, credits? The mere thought was utterly insulting, and more than a little hurtful. She might have been able to stir up more outrage over everything if she wasn't so fucking scared.

Serra had just arrived back on Earth after a long voyage from Alpha Station: X20 when she and her two guards had been taken into custody. Her first reaction had been a mixture of confusion and irritation, but after she had been shown into the interrogation room, that had turned to fear.

She'd been doing upgrades on the shielding of all the outposts between X20 to Earth, making sure that each station located in Alliance territory was well protected. She had built the system, and adding additional layers to the shield ensured that everyone remained safe.

It was a duty she took very seriously.

It was her technology, and no one knew the specs or algorithms like she did. Traveling so much was draining, but it was necessary for her to be onsite to do the calibrations, so she dealt with it. The good thing was that the upgrades took very little time to install, giving her time to work on her other projects during the long journey from station to station.

Serra knew she could get lost in her work, and she was grateful that her mother didn't complain…too much. Since she'd begun traveling, Tania had insisted on accompanying Serra. At first, Serra had been too young to argue, but over the years they had fallen into a companionable understanding. Tania made sure Serra remembered to eat and took care of the day-to-day details that she didn't want to be bothered with.

Due to her status, Serra was often treated like an honored guest wherever they went. She didn't care about the pomp and fuss, but her mother enjoyed the benefits bestowed upon them wherever they went. At times having her mother with her was a strain on Serra's nerves. They didn't really see eye-to-eye on many issues, but Serra knew she needed someone to take care of the small things that allowed her to focus on her work. Sure, she could have simply hired an assistant to take care of those things, but Tania was basically her only family, so it was important to Serra to try and keep that connection, no matter how tenuous it was, and Tania's own assistant took care of most of the details anyways.

When Serra had scheduled her trip back to Earth, she had felt a little guilty because she knew a part of her needed a break from her mother. Tania Lysander-Dobbs wouldn't set foot back on Earth if there was any chance she would run into Serra's fathers. Throughout the years, Serra had heard countless stories about how horrible it had been for Tania to be claimed by General Cade Lysander and General Andrew Dobbs. Her mother had a tendency to exaggerate, but after neither man had come after her, Serra assumed that what Tania had said was true.

There was a price to pay for being a scroll.

When a woman was chosen, the two elite soldiers that claimed her would have their initials tattooed on the left side of her face, marking her as theirs for the world to see. In return, the men would have a similar tattoo placed on their left neck, shoulder and arm as a sign of pride to have claimed a woman. These markings took the place of archaic symbols such as wedding bands to declare them a bonded unit…if there was love within the pairing.

There was no love between Serra's parents, and there never had been. Serra's fathers had never gotten the bonding tattoos. Theirs had been an arranged bonding, an alliance of three powerful families that was more for political gain than anything else. Growing up, Serra was never very close to either of her fathers. Even as a young girl, she knew that no one really understood her, and it became clear that her entire family saw her as an oddity.

After receiving the enhancements when she turned ten, Serra had known she was an anomaly. When she had scored perfect on her placement tests, the trainers had given her further testing as it became evident her intelligence was far more advanced than most elites. To everyone's surprise, they had discovered that she was able to use more of her brain than others, even with their genetic enhancements. The change made her incredibly intelligent, but it had also made her even more different when all she wanted was to be like everyone else.

27

Serra had never gotten her wish, and it became painfully obvious that she would never be normal. Doctors had diagnosed her with a rare disorder, similar to what used to be called autism back in the past before medical technology had removed such anomalies from genetic coding. The condition had been aggravated due to the genetic enhancements, and there was nothing they could do for her once she had gone through the change.

Her grandparents had cut her out of their lives when she had only been a child. At first they had been proud of her intelligence, but when they discovered she was socially awkward and prone to panic attacks, they had written her off as flawed. Perhaps she was, but it was something she lived with, and had even come to enjoy.

She wasn't like anyone else, and that uniqueness made her special.

But special didn't mean accepted...

Her fathers had never been able to relate to her, not that they had ever really tried. She had simply faded away from them over the years. As she'd matured, they had made no move to reconnect to her. She had thought to try and bridge the gap between them two years ago, but when she had gotten their response saying that they had no place for her in their lives, she'd given up. Cade and Andrew seemed far too busy with their own lives, spending time with their mistress instead of worrying about their chosen or their daughter.

As a child, she'd been terrified that her parents would hand her over to the medical staff. She had heard some doctors say that they wanted to study her brain to find out how she was able to use a portion that they had previously been unable to stimulate. She'd had nightmares for weeks about doctors wanting to cut her open to study her like they had done with the Zyphir after the alien invaders had attacked Earth.

Serra had been relieved when she had been transferred into the Academy in the Capital, where they were better equipped to handle someone with her capabilities. It was there she finally found a place where she'd felt like she belonged, only it wasn't the place…it was with Jax and Sully.

Jax Spartan and Sullivan Archer had been two of the older members at the training facility, and upon her arrival they'd made it clear to the others that she was to be left alone when other recruits wanted to mess with her because of her age. Although they had been tasked with looking out for the new recruits and everyone at that facility followed them without hesitation, it had taken Serra some time to understand she was truly safe with them.

They had become her protectors, her friends and confidants.

It had almost destroyed her when they'd been sent to a space station for their first assignment. Serra had started to write letters to them, forgoing vid messages to tell them of her days on Earth. They wrote back when they could, but Serra used her letters to them as a sort of diary, allowing her to write her feelings and thoughts down when she had such a difficult time expressing them to others. She'd liked knowing that Jax and Sully knew about her life and what she was doing. It made her feel closer to them, even though she was light years away, and it gave her the illusion that she wasn't so alone.

When they had come back to Earth when she was sixteen, her feelings for them had changed. As a child she had never seen them as the young men they were, but when they came back she got her first taste of lust. Despite what her mother had told her about being claimed, seeing them again had allowed Serra to dream about what it could be like to be bonded with two men she truly cared for.

For one glorious year after they were back on Earth, it had been like they had never left. When they weren't on duty they would visit her at the Academy. They would often bring her little gifts that she would hide away, and still cherished to this day. It had been almost comical how two of the strongest, most commanding elite soldiers had started to court her. To the outside world Jax and Sully were men to be feared, but they were gentle with her and never hesitated to show her how much they cared.

She had fallen in love with both Jax and Sully before she ever even knew what love really was, and when her mother had torn her away from them, she had been devastated. Because she was underage, she had to abide by her mother's wishes when Tania had taken her off planet. She had always known she would make it back to Jax and Sully one day, but over the years it hadn't happened.

Something had changed.

Serra wasn't sure how it had happened, but Jax and Sully had faded from her life. She had tried to write to them for a while, but after they had stopped responding, she had given up sending the messages and simply stored them in her data files. She enjoyed her life of traveling. Her work was challenging and kept her busy. Still, she'd wanted to reach out to them, but every time she thought about it, she felt a little sick. Her heart would race and her head would begin to throb with a massive headache.

Every year she arranged to have time away from her mother and her work to attend the Freedom Day Gala back on Earth for one simple reason. She wanted to go to Jax and Sully, to seek them out and tell them how much she missed them. But something always stopped her. For some reason she couldn't do it.

Every time she thought about Jax and Archer, the panic would take over, and when she saw them, terror made her flee even as her heart sang at the sight of them. She didn't know what was wrong with her, but she knew something was. Hell, she had even gone as far as getting a med-scan to see if there was some medical reason for her abnormal response to them, but the results hadn't given her any answers. Despite her severe reaction every time she thought of them, she still loved them, even if she couldn't have them.

But she wanted them now.

Desperately.

A hand slammed down on the table, jerking Serra from her thoughts and had fear surging through her. "Ms. Lysander. You have to give us something. If you keep stonewalling us, there will be nothing we can do to help you when official charges are filed," High Commander Newgate ordered.

"I don't know what you want from me," Serra whispered. "I told you, I don't know anything. I don't know what else I can say."

Whenever she got agitated to the point of having a panic attack, she knew she needed certain things to help her combat the fear. She needed to find a quiet place where she felt safe and could refocus herself. Even better would be to wrap herself in her gravity cloak and curl up in a corner somewhere until the dread faded.

She needed to get the hell out of that room before she completely lost her shit.

"I need a moment…"

"Ms. Lysander. This would all go quicker if you just answer our questions," Regent Wyland-Ross said, sympathy showing in her eyes.

"I can't answer what I don't know!"

"You know something!" High Commander Newgate accused. "You're not leaving here until we find out what you're hiding."

Serra knew she was in trouble as her breath began coming in harsh gasps as the terror spiked through her. Buzzing sounded in her ears as her vision blurred. Damn it, damn it, she knew she was headed toward a full-blown attack, and if High Commander Newgate and Regent Wyland-Ross didn't know about her condition they could see her breakdown as guilt.

Please, please god, don't try to touch me.

When she was in full panic mode she couldn't stand having people touch her. She was hypersensitive to most things, and it only got worse when she was in this type of condition. Wrapping her arms around herself tight, she tried to regain some semblance of control as she became light-headed. She began tapping the fingers of each hand to her thumbs in sequence, counting silently in an attempt to calm herself with the gesture she had learned as a child. Sometimes it worked, sometimes it didn't. If she couldn't regain some control, soon she wouldn't be aware of anything around her.

She was dangerous if that happened and would react without thinking.

"Ms. Lysander?"

Regent Wyland-Ross stood and started around the table as the door burst open.

"Don't touch her!"

Serra turned her head and blinked rapidly. As if they'd heard her silent plea, Jax and Sully stormed into the room. Ignoring the others, they came to her, and she knew they could see how precariously close she was to losing herself to the hysterical blindness that could consume her. She wanted to tell them how happy she was to see them, how much she needed them there with her, but the words were locked in her throat that had all but closed as the muscles of her body locked up.

"Commander Spartan, Commander Archer. That door was locked. You're not authorized to interrupt this interrogation," High Commander Newgate bit out in a harsh tone.

Ignoring him, Sullivan Archer yanked Serra's chair to the side so he could kneel in front of her. Gripping her chin he raised her head so she was staring into beautiful light-brown eyes. Just the sight of them calmed her more than anything else could.

"Hello, hummingbird. Just breathe. I'm here. Nothing is going to hurt you."

She focused on Sully as pain surged through her head. It hurt to look at him, but she couldn't seem to look away. She *needed* to see him. Needed him there with her.

High Commander Newgate made a move to push Archer away, but Jax shoved him back before he could get close.

"Commander Spartan, you are very close to being brought up on charges."

Jax ignored the cold fury in High Commander Newgate's voice. "You can't touch her when she's in this state. She'll react without thinking and lash out. If you read her goddamn file, you would've known that."

32

High Commander Newgate relaxed at the reminder. "Yes, I did. You're right."

"I'm sorry," Regent Wyland-Ross said softly, shaken herself for almost making such a costly error. "I shouldn't have tried to touch her, but I just wanted to make sure she was okay."

"Archer and I will see to her."

"You shouldn't be in here," High Commander Newgate said, but the heat of anger had faded.

Jax's deadly smile would have made a lesser man shiver with fear. "Serra Lysander is ours to protect. And we will, from anyone. Even you. We claim her."

He ignored High Commander Newgate's curse and Regent Wyland-Ross' sharp inhale, and turned at the sound of Archer's voice. It was low, but there was a sense of urgency in it that instantly alarmed Jax.

"Jax. Something's wrong."

Dismissing everyone else, Jax quickly squatted down next to Archer so he could look into Serra's eyes. Damn, the impact of those light-green eyes seared straight through to his soul. He could see that they were glazed with pain and fear, but there was something else shining back at him. There was relief. Relief at seeing him and Archer. She should have known they would come to her when she needed them.

This woman owned them.

And now they would own her as well.

"She's in pain, but I don't know why," Archer whispered as he reached up to wipe away the sweat beading her brow. "Something is really wrong. This isn't just a panic attack."

"What is it, son?"

Gone was the powerful regent, replaced by a concerned father as Jax felt a hand grip his shoulder. "I don't know. Get a med tech in here. Now!"

Jax didn't look away from Serra as he barked out the order. The sound of scrambling feet behind him assured him that help was coming, but seeing the pain in her eyes was making him crazy. Beside him, Archer ripped off his uniform top and wrapped it carefully around her shoulders when she began to shake.

Serra winced as she raised a hand up to touch her fingers to her temple and Jax grabbed her other hand, gripping it tight in his own. Fingers wrapped around his like a vise, as if she were desperate to hold onto something. Her skin was cool to the touch, and he could feel her trembling increase. "What is it, sweetheart?"

"Don't…know…head hurts…"

"Everything is going to be okay. We'll take care of you. You know we will. You belong to us, Serra. Do you deny it?"

The throbbing in Serra's head was making it hard to think, but she was aware enough to give him a small smile. "There is no denying it. Jax, I—"

Her words were cut off. The moment she said his name, stars exploded behind her eyes, making her cry out. She heard Jax and Sully both let out savage curses as she pitched forward in her chair. Her body never hit the ground as she felt Jax's strong arms surrounding her, cradling her against his hard body. Unable to combat the pain any longer, she let the darkness claim her, knowing they would watch over her and keep her safe.

Serra woke slowly, drifting in a sea of serenity that only came from being on some sort of drug. For once, her mind was blessedly calm. Thoughts and equations that usually ran through her head like some sort of ticker were missing, chased away by whatever treatment she had been given.

Her eyelids where heavy, and she gave up trying to open her eyes, content to just relax on the gel-bed she was laying on. From the smell in the room, she assumed it meant she was in a medical center. Normally, she would have started to freak out at finding herself there, but she knew she was safe with Jax and Sully.

Despite her confusion, she was sure of that to her very core.

She mentally paused as she thought about them without feeling any pain in her head. God, how long had it been since that had happened? Silently amused, she thought she might have to stock up on whatever the med-techs had given her to combat the throbbing headaches she usually got.

Letting her mind drift, Serra felt a heavy weight over her body that added to her sense of safety, and knew without looking that Jax and Sully had placed a weighted blanket on her. They knew from back when they were young that such things helped her center herself and calmed her. Hearing low voices in the room, a fissure of alarm shot through her, but she settled again as she recognized the familiar cadence of Sully's voice.

"Thanks for coming, Dom."

"No thanks needed. This is some shit you've gotten yourself into, you know."

"We know it, and that's why we asked you to come." Jax's voice was brisk, but there was a warmth in his tone that Serra knew he only used with friends and people he trusted. "The medicals can't find what's wrong with Serra, but we know something is making her head hurt to the point that she passed out earlier. Arik, we need you to help us figure out what that is."

There was a long pause, then a new voice spoke. It was deep, masculine, and so beautiful Serra felt like she was blessed just hearing it. She had heard voices like that before, and knew whoever it belonged to had to be of the D'Aire race.

"I would be happy to aid you anyway that I can, but I will not truth test her without her consent. It is not my way. I will not do it without her permission, even for you, my friend."

"She'll consent."

This time hearing the arrogance in Jax's voice made her smile a little.

"What are you smiling at, hummingbird?"

Serra pried her eyes open and met the brilliant whiskey color of Sully's as he looked down at her. The endearment he had pinned her with when she was young due to her propensity to tap her fingers made her smile. "Can I have—"

Before she could finish her request, he held up a small cup with a straw sticking out of it. She took the straw into her mouth gratefully and took a long pull of the cool, refreshing liquid. She wanted to smile again as the taste of her favorite juice hit her taste buds and drank more down greedily.

Archer set the cup back down on the side table and picked up her hand, needing the connection with her. She looked so small on the stark white gel-bed. The elevated medical console over the center of her body made it impossible to sit down next to her, when all he wanted to do was snatch her up into his arms so he could keep her safe from anything, everything.

In all his life, Serra was the one thing he had wanted that had eluded him. He ached for her until he thought he would go mad. He searched her face, studying her as satisfaction filled him at seeing Jax and his mark near her eye that told the world she belonged to them.

They had claimed her.

It was an action that both he and Jax had been in complete accord with, and one that could get them court-martialed if she brought them up for sanctions. After Serra had gone down in the interrogation room, they'd been ordered away from her. With no claim on her and without authority over the investigation, they would have been banned from her.

And that was something they wouldn't have allowed.

Before the med-techs had arrived, Archer had used the device he had brought with him to the security center. Hearing she was in custody had made him take the marking device with him when he got the call. It had only taken a few seconds as he'd touched the device to the left side of her face, instantly transferring the tattoo on her skin, but the result made her theirs for the rest of their lives. The stylized pattern was a combination of both his and Jax's initials, comprised of a scrolling design so that it complimented the scroll mark on the right side of her face that classified her as a fertile female.

"You had us worried, sweetheart," Jax said from where he was standing on the other side of the bed. The gruff sound of his voice didn't seem to bother Serra, as was evident from the smile playing on her lush lips.

"Sorry. What happened?"

Jax's jaw tightened at the weak sound of her voice. He didn't like seeing her lying there looking so helpless. "You passed out in the interrogation room. They have you on some sort of blocker now, but they can't figure out what triggered your attack."

"We've brought some friends with us that may be able to help you," Archer added.

Serra smiled up at him, then reached out to take Jax's hand so she was holding onto both men. It felt so good to have them with her again. She'd missed them so much, but amazingly, she still felt like she knew them. Over the years, she'd tried to keep tabs on them, in her own way. She knew they were both dedicated to their positions in the Alliance—just as she was—but it touched her heart that they had come to her at the first sign of trouble.

"Before that happens, we need to ask her a few questions."

A tall, muscular man moved into view. He was wearing the standard grey uniform of an elite, but the two metal bars on his lapel designated him as a director instead of the four bars both Jax and Archer wore as commanders. Serra barely held back a shiver as eyes black as midnight bore into her from a harsh face that could have been chiseled from marble. Dominic Stryker was a handsome man, but there was a lethal edge to him that made her think he was dangerous. Something about him made her extremely uncomfortable.

"Serra, this is Dominic Stryker, the Director of Security and Interrogation here in the Capital."

"Ms. Lysander, I need to know if you would like Commanders Spartan and Archer brought up on charges."

She felt more than saw Jax and Sully tense, but she didn't understand the cold statement. Even though it had been a long time since she had been able to spend time with them, she would never do anything to hurt Jax and Sully. Ever.

"Why would I do that?"

"Your records state that you have been given exempt status. They claimed you while you were unable to protest. Your status allowed you to choose your own bonding unit."

They'd claimed her? Her heart gave a hard thump of joy even as the insistent throbbing in her head began again. The medical console beeped in warning as it picked up the change in her vitals.

"Damn it, what is that? What's wrong? Dom, get the doctor in here. Now."

She heard the fear Jax masked behind his barking command, then saw Jax's father step forward to place a calming hand on his son's arm. "You can't blame the poor girl for being upset, Jax. Stars, it's bad enough that you claimed her while she was unconscious. I tell you, when your mother finds out, she is going to skin you alive."

Jax shot his father a glare. "She won't find out."

Regent Spartan snorted. "Of course she will. That woman knows everything."

"You better hope she doesn't. Or else she might also find out you're the one who ordered her daughter-in-law into interrogation."

Serra wanted to laugh at the pained expression that settled over Regent Spartan's face, but another man stepped forward, claiming her attention. The newcomer was taller than the other men in the room, and so beautiful, it almost hurt to look at him. He had an innate sensuality that hit her like a psychic punch. His long white-blond hair was pulled back at the temples, leaving his perfect face free of encumbrances. Iridescent blue eyes stared down at her, swirling with sympathy and a calm so soothing that it helped her center herself again.

This new male was one of the D'Aire race. Humans had nicknamed them *Angels* due to the majestic wings they could spring from their backs. They could call forth the wings at will, but like now, often kept them hidden using the magic of their species. Serra had been to the home planet of the D'Aire many times, and had a deep respect for their people.

"Greetings to you, one of the light," she said the formal greeting of his race and watched as his lips curved in a small smile. He gave a slight bow of his head.

"Greetings to you as well, little one. I am Arik of the V'Dir clan."

Serra thought that Arik and Dom looked comical standing next to one another. It was like looking at the devil standing next to an angel. Arik had a lean body compared to Dominic's stockier build, but both of them were packed with muscle that would warn anyone that they'd be formidable opponents.

"Whatever is ailing her is not something your medical technology can counter. I can sense a blank space in her mind, even standing over here. If I am right, her memory has been altered and that is what's causing her pain."

"What does that mean?" Archer demanded, but Arik didn't look away from Serra. He took a step forward, only stopping when Jax put a hand on his chest.

"Explain."

Arik tore his gaze away from Serra, and looked at the barely restrained fury on Jax and Archer's faces. They were her protectors, her bonded. In the D'Aire culture they would be called the *keepers of her heart*. Of course they would require an explanation.

They all would.

Chapter Three

"Help me up."

At Serra's request, Jax moved the medical console down toward the foot of the bed as Sully raised the gel-bed so she was sitting up. She felt better, more stable being able to see everyone. Gripping the weighted blanket to her chest, she focused her attention on the D'Aire, but remained acutely aware of the two men by her sides. "You're talking about *xili*, aren't you?"

"I am."

"What the hell is *xili*?" Jax demanded.

Arik let out a sigh, then shifted his position so he could address everyone. They were in a private room in the medical center, which was good since the less people that had the information he was about to give, the better. Everyone in the room had been implanted with the language converter chip that allowed them to understand the different languages of the races, but then again, so had most of the medical staff in the center.

Director Dominic Stryker may have been the lowest ranking member in the room, but Arik trusted him implicitly. When Arik sent him a look, Dom nodded and strode over to the door and shut it, ensuring privacy for their conversation. Regents Spartan and Wyland-Ross, as well as High Commander Newgate could be trusted. It helped that Arik could pick up on nuances of someone's character when he touched them, so he was assured of that.

The D'Aire had the ability to slip into someone's mind and do a scan, although it was against their code to do so without permission. Still, for an older D'Aire like Arik, it was almost impossible not to pick up impressions just being around someone. Sensing Serra's tumultuous emotions, Arik had felt something else in the chaos.

Something that he hadn't sensed in years, and it disturbed him to a level he couldn't even begin to describe.

41

Sensing the impatience flowing off of Jax and Archer, Arik knew it was time for answers. "I believe I need to begin with some background to explain this. Years ago, before the D'Aire knew of Earth, we had made contact with the Helios when we traveled to Helix. Although they had welcomed us and we have good relations with them still, there were things back then that were…troubling to us."

"Troubling how?" High Commander Newgate asked.

"As you now know, it is a world that is primarily jungle, and its people are wild. No matter how civilized they seem, there is a feral quality to them if provoked. That feral quality also applies to their home world. Their jungle is not some place you ever want to venture unescorted. Back then there were also several plant specimens that worried us when we saw the effects of them at work. Over time, most of those have been eradicated, but there are always a few that slip through the cracks. I sense something in Serra that I haven't felt in a very long time. If I'm right, she has been tainted with *xili*."

"It's a mind-altering drug used to implant suggestions into the user," Serra explained before anyone could ask. "I've studied it. I've read a lot about different flora and fauna species of the planets I've visited, but I've never taken *xili*. Especially not after knowing the side effects of the drug. That is to say, if I could even find it. Even then, I wouldn't take it."

"Not knowingly," Jax said, his voice deadly quiet. He focused his steel-grey eyes on Arik. "You're saying you think someone fucked with her mind, aren't you? How can you tell?"

"Only the D'Aire are able to sense the void left in someone who has been tainted by *xili*."

"Why weren't we told about your ability if this drug is a threat to us?" Regent Wyland-Ross demanded.

"It isn't something that is commonly known, and we have thought the drug had been destroyed long ago."

"Apparently, you were wrong," High Commander Newgate said, then he sighed. "This is a clusterfuck of epic proportions if there has been a resurgence of this damn drug."

"This is a nightmare," Regent Wyland-Ross agreed. "We're already dealing with a crisis with the stealth technology, now this? We could all be in danger."

"Well, it's not like that is anything new. Why would today be any different?" Archer asked.

Regent Wyland-Ross was not amused. "This isn't a joke, Commander Archer."

"Of course it isn't, but I wouldn't feel normal if someone wasn't trying to kill me on a daily basis," Archer added dryly. "I wouldn't know what to do with myself otherwise."

"You have a very twisted sense of humor, Archer," Regent Spartan said, frowning.

"He always did," Serra said, smiling up at him.

Regent Spartan shook his head at them. "We need to have a meeting with Ambassador Tala of Helix and Ambassador M'Dor about this. This could damage all our species if someone is using this to control people."

Arik nodded. "It would be recommended. Ambassador M'Dor would be well aware of the ramifications."

"What does this mean for Serra? Is this dangerous for her?" Jax asked, gripping Serra's hand in his as if he wanted to shield her from anything that would dare harm her.

"I know you called me here to ask me to perform a truth test, but there is a way to counteract the drug…"

"Then do it," Archer ordered.

"It isn't that simple. I can aid you," Arik said softly to Serra. "But only if you consent to it, and you must be sure. You would have to let me do a mind scan so we can discover what was done to you. It will be difficult for both of us, but it could be very dangerous if you fight me."

Serra struggled to understand what Arik was telling her. Logic. She was good at logic, and she stamped down her own emotions so she could focus on what needed to be done. "Do it."

"Wait a damn minute," Jax demanded. "If this could be dangerous—"

"I won't fight him," Serra said. "I need to do this. If someone messed with my head, I want to know. I *need* to know. I always knew something was wrong, but I didn't know what it was. I've been to medical for tests before, and they could never find anything, but I knew. Every time I think of you and Sully my head hurts. That's not normal, Jax."

Jax let out a vicious curse. "I'm going to be very pissed if something happens to you."

"Gee, you pissed?" Archer said drolly. "What would that be like?"

Jax glared at him, but Serra surprised them both by laughing. "You two haven't changed a bit."

"We need the room cleared if we're going to do this," Arik ordered softly.

"We stay," Jax said in a low voice, daring him to argue.

Instead, Arik nodded. "As her bonded, you and Archer should remain, but everyone else will have to go. That is, if you accept them as your bonded."

Serra looked at Jax and Sully, and smiled despite the pain her head. "I do."

"Dom, this will take all my energy and I will need you to help me after."

"Done."

"We'll go set up that meeting with the Ambassadors," Regent Spartan said. Before he left, he moved to the bed and lightly touched his fingers to the back of Serra's hand that Jax held. "Welcome to our family, my dear. We're very happy to have you."

"Thank you," Serra replied, emotions making her voice waver.

44

After the regents and High Commander Newgate left the room, Archer turned back to Arik. "So, how do you do this?"

"I will need to follow Serra back into her memories to find out when she was tainted. Once the memory is retrieved, any affects should dissipate."

"Should? As in there is no guarantee this will work?"

"Things such as this rarely come with a guarantee. Going into someone else's mind is difficult to do when the individual isn't the Keeper of a D'Aire. This is why it is rarely done."

"Is there a risk to you doing this?" Dom demanded. He shot a hand out to stop Archer from speaking. "I have been entrusted with his safety while he's on Earth. I get that you want to help your woman, but we can't put a goddamn D'Aire Ambassador in jeopardy either."

"I'll be fine. This is my choice."

"Serra, are you sure you want to do this?" Jax asked.

"Positive."

Arik placed a hand on Jax's shoulder. "I'm sorry, my friend, but neither of you can touch her while we do this. I cannot risk getting readings from you as well."

Archer leaned down and brushed his lips against the claiming mark near Serra's eye. "Even if we can't touch you, we are with you."

"I know."

Serra smiled at Archer as he moved back to stand next to Dom at the end of the bed. Jax gripped her chin, turning her head toward him. There was a fire burning in his grey eyes that made her belly flutter with nerves while her head pounded with pain. "We will fix this."

"That's what I'm hoping. It really sucks feeling like my head is going to explode all the time."

"Think about us that often do you?"

"Yes," she whispered.

His eyes narrowed with determination. "It will be done. Whatever it takes, we'll find a way to make you better." With that, he leaned down and pressed his lips to hers in a kiss so tender it brought tears to her eyes.

Serra felt pain shoot into her head, but held onto Jax when he tried to pull back. This was her first real kiss. Pain be damned, she wanted his lips on hers. He gently removed her hands from where they were gripping his uniform jacket, and pulled back to stroke his fingers lightly over the tattoo of their initials. She watched his eyes flicker with agony as he let go of her, then watched them harden as he signaled to Arik.

"We are trusting you with her."

"Understood. We will need complete silence while we do this."

"We won't bother you. We would never risk her, or you. Thank you for this."

Arik smiled. "You may thank me after we know it has worked."

Gripping her hands together so she wouldn't fidget, Serra forced herself to remain still. Her mind was churning with thousands of thoughts. Logic, she told herself again. She needed to approach this exercise logically. It was the only way she would get through this.

Arik sat down on the bed beside her, those patient iridescent eyes calming her again. "I need you to relax. Calm your mind, and let me lead you where we need to go."

"I'm sorry, I'm nervous," she blurted out. "I'm a woman of science. I know about the things your people are capable of, but I have a difficult time understanding how you can lead me anywhere in my mind."

"We are going to travel back through your memories to retrieve what you have lost. There is a memory hidden there of when you were tainted with the *xili*. Once we see what really happened, whatever suggestion was put in place will no longer be effective."

Her lips pursed in anger at the thought that someone had done that to her. "Let's do this then."

Arik reached out and placed three fingers on each side of her head over her temples. Looking into his glowing blue eyes she felt like she was drowning for a moment. Suddenly, it was as if she were thrown back into time. A million thoughts shifted through her brain at light speed, making her throat burn with the need to scream out as the pain in her head increased.

Then it stopped.

Serra found herself drifting through her own memories, back through the years as Arik searched for the blank spot he'd sensed. It wasn't like thinking back on something that had happened before. No, this was like seeing her own memories through Arik's eyes. It was strange. Left her feeling off-balance and unsettled. Pushing aside her own emotional response, she tried to pay attention to what she was seeing in a clinical manner and let him lead the way.

The images had a weird feel to them, as if she were looking through a camera that was slightly out of focus. She was fascinated by the experience, then a jolt shot through her as she realized exactly what she was seeing.

It was her, sitting in some sort of chair in a dark room. There were straps attached to her wrists and ankles, holding her tied to the chair so she couldn't move. She was young, so young. Serra could tell she was around seventeen, but she had no memory of the scene.

That terrified her.

"*Calm,*" Arik whispered softly into her head.

She held onto the sound of his voice like she would have a life preserver at sea, reminding herself that she was not alone. She surveyed the room her younger self was in, and shock filled her to see she was in some sort of castle made of dark stone. She glanced at the wide window, out at the black sky that was filled with clouds that turned a hot, searing red as lightning crackled through the air. Red and black sky…there was only one place that she knew of had a red and black sky, but she had never been there.

Not that she remembered.

Known as the Dark Planet, Tartarus sat at the edge of Alliance regulated space. Aptly named for its frequent electrical storms and volatile inhabitants, Tartarus was a hostile world. The Tarins were known as the Lords of War, and were a barbaric, demon-like race that fed off the energy of others. They lived off the blood-lust they got when in battle, or the energy and strength they received during sexual release.

These energy vampires existed under a feudal system. Centuries ago, the Tarins had gone to war with Earth, but their swords were no match for humans and their more advanced weaponry. For years after the war, the Tarins had closed off their planet, choosing to remain isolated instead of allow interference of any other species. Now, the Tarins held a tentative truce with the Alliance, although they were still considered a hostile ally. The Alliance traded with the Tarins for a mineral they had on their planet that was used for high-powered jump drives installed in Alliance space vessels.

Because the Tarins were still fighting a civil war, all visitors were carefully documented. There was only one Alliance colony on Tartarus, nicknamed the Hades Outpost, and it was almost impossible to get clearance to visit the planet. There was a faction of lords who prided themselves on their harems of slaves, while the other half fought for the equality needed to officially have a treaty with the Alliance.

It was a dangerous place to be, and Serra had a hard time reconciling that she had ever been there. She knew that people often tried to visit the planet due to the Tarins reputation for sexual prowess. Sex with a Tarin was supposed to be extremely intense, but anyone was at risk of disappearing into the dark void, never to be seen again. Kidnapping and slavery were still alarming issues that would only be stopped once the civil war came to an end.

"Are you sure about this?"

Serra's attention turned to the deep voice of the man who had spoken. No, not a man. This was a Tarin male. He stood at a little over seven feet tall and his eyes were completely black, making them look like deep pits of darkness set in his face. He was dressed in all black, and she could see he was muscular despite the black armor-like plate he wore over his broad chest.

"I am. This has to be done."

Pain surged through her as Serra recognized her mother's voice. Tania moved into view and Serra's blood ran cold at the sight of her. She was wearing a blood-red dressing gown, tied at the waist. Tania Lysander-Dobbs was a beautiful woman, and her hair was disheveled as if she had just gotten out of bed. Serra watched as Tania went to the Tarin male and felt her stomach roll as he gripped her mother hard by the hair.

"You are one sick female. I think I like that about you. It is not often I have come across a mother who would scar her offspring with such a memory simply to keep you in coins."

"It's not just that. I'm doing this for her."

"Do not lie to me, human. You have paid with both your coin and your body, so I will uphold my part of the bargain."

"Did you give her the drug?"

"Aye, she is tainted with the *xili*. Now that she is fully awakened, you may implant what you need into her head. I will bring in my slaves."

Serra felt more than saw Arik next to her. "*Try to calm yourself. This is but a memory, and cannot hurt you.*"

But he was wrong. Memories could hurt. She tried to do what he suggested and could sense him lending her his strength as she watched her mother—her one family member she had trusted—lean down near her younger self's ear and lie.

"You'll see what bonding can do to you. How horrible, how painful it is. You'll be afraid. Learn to fear it. There is no room in your life for Jax Spartan and Sullivan Archer. No room for any man. Claiming will only bring you pain."

The Tarin male came back with two others who held a young woman by the arms. The woman struggled, crying and begging to be set free. The Tarin male walked over to join Tania, gripping her hard by her hair again. "They will put on a show that will program your offspring to never seek a consort. Now, come. I have another use for you."

"I paid you already."

"You will pay again."

Thankfully, the Tarin male pulled Serra's mother out of view as he jerked on the tie to her robe. Horror filled Serra as she watched the other two Tarin males throw the young woman on the bed, ripping at her clothes as they attacked her. The sound of her screams filled the room and Serra's head.

The scene disappeared in an instant, but the disturbing images haunted Serra. Arik turned her into him, shielding her from the terrible memory. *"That is enough. You know why you fear it now. It is over."*

"How could she? How could anyone do something like that?"

She was sobbing inside, weeping for the loss of all she had known. The mother she'd thought loved her, and the time that had been lost with Jax and Archer. Both had been taken from her with a betrayal so grievous she might never fully recover.

Arik was a small comfort as he was still joined in her head. She could feel the fatigue dragging her down, but he stirred in her mind, silently asking her to hold on.

"I know that this is difficult for you, but perhaps I can give you something that will help ease your pain."

She couldn't imagine what could possibly help her after witnessing the monstrous treachery her mother had committed, but she mentally blinked in surprise as Arik began sharing some of his own memories with her. It was a collection of the years she'd been kept away from Jax and Sully. Arik had been friends with them for a long time, and he generously shared each time either Jax or Sully had spoken of her over the years. Each snippet was short, but there were many, and seeing them did help heal her heart that felt as if it had been ripped into pieces.

When the show was over, she felt exhausted. "*Thank you for that.*"

"*Rest now, little one. All will be well when you awaken. There will be no pain to keep you from Jax and Archer.*"

No, pain in her head had disappeared, but the ache in her heart remained. She would have to deal with that later, though. She gave herself over to the black abyss, needing the escape, and prayed that dreams wouldn't follow her into sleep.

Chapter Four

Archer stared down at Serra as she slept in their bed.

It had been almost twenty-four hours since she had passed out in the medical center, but Arik had assured them that she was physically unharmed by the mind scan he'd done. Both Archer and Jax had been adamant about taking her out of the medical center and bringing her home so she could rest properly, wanting her to wake in comfort rather than the clinical setting of medical. Since she had accepted them as her bonded, they had every right to make that call.

Fury filled Archer at the thought of what they'd discovered in the mind scan that Arik had performed. Tania Lysander-Dobbs would pay for her treachery, and she would pay dearly. Archer's heart had ached when he'd listened to Arik's recounting of the memory Serra had repressed due to the *xili* she'd been drugged with. So many years had been stolen from them, but they would make up for them.

It was a vow that Archer and Jax were determined to fulfill.

He and Jax had luxurious quarters in one of the most secure buildings in the heart of the Capital. When they'd moved in, they had each claimed a wing of the top floor in the large, multi-tiered suite for their own use, with common areas they shared on the middle floor of the residence. The lower floor housed the gym and a large pool that they both used religiously.

In the center of the top floor, they'd had a large bedroom built they knew would one day belong to their chosen. Serra. The room had always been meant for her, and seeing her in it brought a lightness to Archer's heart that he hadn't felt in years.

She was truly theirs now.

With her needs in mind, they had decorated the room with muted shades of lavender and black, knowing that she did better in environments with soft, basic colors. The pale shade of purple was her favorite color, and the light beige matting on the floor was soft to walk on and also gave the added benefit of muffling any sounds that may disturb her in her sanctuary.

Archer sat on the side of the bed, then he pulled back the covers so he could lie down next to Serra. She barely stirred as he pulled her gently into his arms and tucked the gravity blanket around her more securely. For so many years Archer had dreamed about her, wondering if she had forgotten the bond they'd had, but she had accepted them without hesitation, even with her head throbbing from the insidious programming her mother had tried to force on her. He was content feeling her against him, and he smiled as she snuggled closer.

It was where she belonged.

"Sully…"

He glanced down at Serra's face to see a small smile creased her lips even though her eyes were still closed. "How did you know it was me?"

Her thick lashes fluttered before they opened, and her light-green eyes met his. "Who else besides you or Jax would be in bed with me?"

"Good answer. But it could have been Jax."

Serra smiled at him. "You smell different. Jax has a spicy scent, while you smell clean and earthy."

"Earthy? Is that a good thing?"

"It is." Serra could feel her cheeks heat at waking up next to him. She wasn't used to having a man in her bed. Hell, she really wasn't used to a man around at all. The only males she was ever around were her assistants or her guards, and they faded into the background most of the time so she barely noticed them. She tried to pull away from Archer, but he held her still. "I need to use the facilities."

"Of course." Bounding out of the bed, he scooped her up in his arms and carried her into the bathroom. She blushed again as she realized she was no longer wearing the plain white shirt and pants

54

all patients wore in the medical center. Instead, she was wearing a pretty gray nightgown made of a thin, shimmering fabric she knew was only found on the D'Aire home planet. One of them had to have changed her. She wasn't embarrassed about her body. In fact, she had a very healthy attitude toward nudity, but it was different now knowing they were her bonded.

She looked at him expectantly after he set her down in the lavish bathroom. After a long pause, she shooed him toward the door with one of her hands. He simply crossed his arms and frowned. "I don't think I should leave you alone. You might still be weak."

She couldn't help but admire the way his muscles bulged under his cream-colored shirt, but she wasn't going to let that sway her. "I'll be fine. I'd like some privacy please."

He sighed. "Fine. Take all the time you need. I'll run downstairs and get you something to eat." He pointed to a panel on the wall. "Use this intercom if you need me."

"Thank you."

Once she was alone, she took care of her more pressing needs, then looked around the bathroom that was perfect for three people living together. What she had seen from the bedroom and now the bathroom, it was apparent that Jax and Sully lived very well as commanders. The bathroom was a huge space, with a black floor and pale, lavender colored walls and three small additional rooms that housed the toilets. At the far end of the room was a large, white tub surrounded by glass walls. There were three steps down into the tub, and she could see from the many showerheads within the space that it was also a shower.

In the main section of the bathroom there were two countertops across from each other with black sinks set into the white counters, two on one side with a single large one on the other. Over the sinks were mirrors with muted lights glowing around the edges. Moving to the side with the single sink, she opened the vanity mirror and saw all of the products she'd had in her bags when she arrived back on Earth.

Obviously, someone had delivered her things when she'd been sleeping.

Her muscles ached from inactivity, telling her she had been sleeping for a long time. Taking out a small rectangular box, she opened the lid of her new nano-cleanser prototype and inserted the nozzle into her mouth. She pressed the button and seconds later, felt much better when her mouth was minty and clean. The nano-cleanser was perfect for space travel, since the nano technology cleaned without the need for water. It was something she had invented on her down time and wasn't her usual type of experiment, but if she was right—and she usually was—the nano-cleaner would be a big seller. It would be nice to be able to share the profits with her assistant for helping with it. She might not need the credits, but he could use them.

Needing some time to assimilate everything that had happened, she made sure the door to the bathroom was closed before walking further into the room. She pressed the panel to turn on the shower and adjusted the temperature. After getting undressed, she stepped down into the glass enclosure, and let the multiple showerheads beat back some of her fatigue.

It made her smile to see her favorite citrus-scented products lined up on a shelf, and she made use of them while she centered her thoughts. She was a claimed woman now, bonded to the two men she had always dreamed about. It was so freeing being able to think about them without her head exploding with pain.

Just the thought of that made her mouth tighten in anger as she rinsed the cleanser out of her hair. What her mother did to her when she was seventeen was unforgiveable. So many years had been wasted, years that could have been spent with Jax and Sully.

All three of them had been cheated.

With them, she had always been accepted. Normal was whatever she wanted it to be, and they had never made her feel as if she lacked anything. Over the years, she had been missing that, never feeling like she truly belonged anywhere or with anyone. That had been taken from her, and for what? Her mother had stolen her chance for happiness because of her own greed, forcing Serra to remain alone and unloved. It was an unconscionable act, and one that Serra would never forgive.

As she finished her shower, Serra thought about what the future held for her, Jax and Sully. There were so many issues they still had to work through, both personally as well as professionally, and to top it all off, there was the matter of the stealth technology that had to be figured out. She had some ideas about how to handle that, but first she would have to talk it over with Jax and Sully before it went any further.

She turned off the water and made her way to the drying chamber instead of using one of the soft towels that hung on the racks. As the warm air swirled around her, she realized she had something to prove to them before they could move on. She was no longer that shy, scared teen Sully and Jax were used to. She was a strong woman, who was known for being blunt to the point that people often cringed when she spoke whatever was on her mind. But this was all new territory for her. Still, she needed to show them that she was a match for them in every way.

Too much time had been wasted, and she was done being restricted from what she wanted most…to be with Sully and Jax. She wanted a life filled with love and laughter. Needed to feel connected to them in a way she'd only been able to in her dreams, where the pain didn't follow. She wanted to touch and to be touched.

And she was done waiting.

With nothing holding her back now, she got out of the drying tube and settled on a plan. She picked up the nightgown, fingering it for a moment before deciding to use the soft, gray robe that hung from a peg on the wall. Tying the belt of the robe after she put it on, she then dropped the nightgown into a bin she found for dirty clothes before heading back into the bedroom.

As she knew he would be, Sully sat on the side of the bed, waiting for her. There was a tray of food next to him, but she couldn't seem to look away from him long enough to see what he'd brought her. He was so beautiful, with his strong body that made her hands ache to touch it. His dark-blond hair was a little longer than what was considered standard for elites, but it was the rebel in him that had never truly been extinguished. She stopped in front of him, just out of reach. Her stomach felt empty, but first she had another hunger to assuage.

"I have some things to say to you," she began then wanted to wince at how cold her voice sounded.

He nodded slowly. "All right."

"First, I want to say thank you for coming to me when you knew I was in trouble. I know it's been a long time since we've actually spent time together."

Sully shook his head. He placed his hands on his knees as if to stop himself from reaching out to her. "It doesn't matter how long it's been, Serra. You matter to us. You always have, and you always will. You don't have to thank me for that."

She blew out a slow breath. "Still, I want you to know that it means a lot to me. I've always been able to depend on you, and it was…difficult for me not to be able to come to you before this."

His face grew hard, and she could see the anger flash in his light-brown eyes. "That wasn't your fault. Your mother will pay for what she did to you."

"She will," she agreed. "Even though we have years to make up for, we're bonded now. I have to tell you that Arik showed me his memories of you. Of both you and Jax."

"He told us. I don't have any problems with that. Neither does Jax." Sully paused for a moment before he spoke again. "I guess now is a good time to confess something to you, too. While you

58

were sleeping we had a look at your data unit. We read the letters you wrote us."

"You…" Confusion flickered through her, and it increased when his voice hardened.

"Serra, we never got those letters. If we knew you wanted us too, we would have come for you long before now."

"But, I sent them. I thought you were angry with me when you stopped writing—"

"We never got them," he said adamantly. "We never knew. When we found the letters we had a tech look at your unit and we found a block had been placed on it."

"That's impossible. I would have known if—"

"Only if you had been looking for it. The block was buried deep, and wouldn't have been caught on a normal scan. Serra, your mother had someone tamper with your unit in order to bounce any communications you tried to send us." He paused again. "We found it also blocked your communications with your fathers as well."

She opened her mouth to protest, then stopped herself. Stars, would her mother's treachery ever end? It all made a horrible sort of sense and she couldn't deny that her mother would have done it to ensure Serra was kept isolated. Pushing her feelings on that aside, she simply said, "Of course she did."

"Come here, hummingbird," he said, reaching out to grip her hands in his to stop her fingers from tapping against the side of her legs. He pulled her closer, so she was standing between his legs.

"I'm sorry, I'm nervous. I've never been in this type of situation. Obviously," she added with a little laugh. "I'm happy you claimed me, though."

His face lit up with a wicked grin that stole her breath. "I'm pretty damn happy we claimed you, too. You must be starving. They said you'd need to eat and rest a lot for the next few days. I brought you some—"

She placed her hands on his shoulders to stop him. "I know we have a lot of things to talk about, and I am hungry, but there is something else I want before we get to that."

"Okay…"

Serra worried her lip with her teeth, trying to figure out how to say what she wanted to him. He noticed her hesitation, and gave her an encouraging smile. "Honey, you don't have to filter yourself with me. Just say whatever it is you want to say."

"I want to have sex."

Archer froze and simply blinked at her. Well, hell. He hadn't been expecting that. Blood surged from his head, straight down to his cock, leaving him feeling a little lightheaded. "Well, that was pretty fucking blunt."

She frowned. "You said not to filter it."

He laughed at that, but the lust heating his blood making it hard to think. Archer sobered, trying to pay attention to the conversation instead of ripping that fucking robe off her and throwing her down on the bed. "Hummingbird, I love your kind of unfiltered, but I don't want to rush you—"

"I think I've waited long enough. But here's the thing. I want both you and Jax, it's just that…"

"Honey, trust me when I say that Jax and I both want you. So much we pretty much can't see straight, but you're a virgin. We're not some assholes that are going to jump you for your first damn time. We each want our own time with you, to show you how special you are to us before both of us join you in here. We can take this at whatever pace you need. We have a lifetime of loving you together."

Serra relaxed a little at that. She did want to be with Jax and Sully, but the thought of being with both of them her first time had been slightly daunting. "I'm glad. From what I've heard from other claimed women, men tend to think it's normal to just rush into the whole ménage thing."

"For women that are used to having two lovers at once, I can see that. But it's important to us for you to know that we will always put your needs first. If Jax and I both took you this first time, we could give you pleasure. More than you've ever experienced before, but it would also be selfish of us to rush you into that."

She silently agreed. Still, she didn't want him thinking she was completely innocent. "I may technically be a virgin, but it's not like I've never experimented before."

His brow rose. "I hope you mean with that little toy we found in your bags, and not with other men."

Damn, she'd forgotten they had unpacked for her. She jerked her chin up and looked him dead in the eyes. "I've never been able to be close to men, but yes, my vibrator helps me sleep at night."

"Stars, I love how you speak your mind, woman. You won't need your toy anymore. We'll take care of your needs from now on."

She arched a brow. "Will you?"

"Oh yeah, we definitely will." He leaned forward and pressed his lips to hers. Serra sighed, letting the pleasure burn through her as he placed his hands on her hips to pull her closer. She wound her arms around his neck when he took the kiss deeper, and let out a soft sigh as their tongues dueled in a passionate play of pleasure. She loved the taste of him, loved the feel his hard body pressed against her.

But it wasn't enough.

She pulled back, breathing hard as she looked into his eyes. "That was my second kiss."

"Do you know how hot it makes me to know that no one else has touched those pretty lips of yours?"

Smiling a little, she rubbed his shoulders nervously. "Well, it was my second kiss that I actually wanted. One of my old guards tried to kiss me, but—" She let out a startled yelp when his hands dug into her hips in a punishing hold.

"Sorry."

"Don't worry. I reported the officer, and he was taken off my detail a few hours later." She shot him a mocking glance. "You wouldn't have had anything to do with that, would you?"

He tried for an innocent expression. "Not me. That was all Jax. Officer Gainer is now stationed at the penal colony on Mars."

That made her laugh. "I bet he is. I knew you two had something to do with his transfer, but I don't want to think about that right now."

"What do you want?"

"I want to see you."

Archer slowly stood up, his body brushing against hers as he did. He felt captivated by her. He wanted to take things slow, but he was already having trouble holding onto his control. He jerked his shirt off, baring his chest to her and her light-green eyes watched him with rapt fascination. From anyone else, that look might seem almost clinical, but he knew her. The more interested in something she was, the more intensely she studied it.

And at the moment her entire focus was on him.

She reached up as if to trace the hard lines of the muscles on his abdomen, but she paused before she made contact.

"Touch me." His voice was a command and a plea all at once. He had to hold back a groan when she did as he'd demanded, and her hands softly began to stroke over his skin. His body felt hot, tight with tension, and his cock felt so hard it could have burst through the fabric of his pants. Needing the relief, he unfastened the tie on his pants and let them drop to the floor, allowing his engorged shaft the freedom to jut out.

Serra hissed out a breath as her eyes widened. "Wow."

He choked back a laugh as he lifted his legs out of the pants and kicked them off to the side. "Real is better than any toy."

Amusement sparkled in her light-green eyes. "Really? My vibrator pulses and expands. Can you really do better than that?"

He let out a growl as he lifted her and took her down onto the bed, covering her body with his. He began to tickle her, making her shriek with laughter. As she struggled beneath him, the belt of her robe came lose, and the fabric parted, exposing her breasts.

They were both breathing hard as Archer cupped one of her breasts in his hand so her nipple poked at the center of his palm. "You are lovely, Serra. More than I even dreamed."

"I never knew lovemaking could be fun."

"It can be anything we want it to be. It can be soft and gentle, or it can be rough and desperate. Nothing is wrong when it comes to how we touch one another."

Serra felt her skin flush under his heated gaze as she parted the robe so it was fully open, exposing her body to him. "Show me. Show me how it can be."

He gently lifted her enough to completely remove the robe and his cock pulsed as he saw the bare mound of her pussy.

"So soft," he murmured as his fingers stroked over her bare skin. She jerked in surprised, but he caught her gasp in his mouth as he kissed her again. His cock was already hard and throbbing to the point of pain, but he wanted to make this good for her.

He needed to make this special.

Shifting lower, he captured the nipple of her right breast in his mouth, tugging lightly at the peak with his teeth.

"Stars, that feels good," she moaned.

He hummed as he suckled her, then switched to the other nipple, moving his hand down to her core so he could stroke his fingertips over the silken folds of her pussy that were already wet with her juices.

"Spread for me, hummingbird. Open these beautiful legs for me so I can show you how good I can make you feel," he whispered.

Serra didn't hesitate as she spread her legs wide for him. Anticipation surged through him, making his mouth water as he saw the glistening flesh of her bare pussy. He settled his body between her parted thighs, and trailed a finger softly over her slit, coating the digit with her dew.

"Do you know what I'm going to do to you, Serra?" he asked as he moved his finger up, circling her clit with a whisper of a touch. "First, I'm going to suck this little bud while I fuck you with my fingers…"

"I'm close already," she warned breathlessly as she shifted her legs wider as if in invitation.

"Good. You're going to come, and come hard so that you soak me with your juice, then I'm going to fill you with my cock. Do you want that, Serra?"

"God, yes. I want you. Want you filling me. Want you—ah!"

Serra cried out as he went to work, his lips closing tight around her clit as he pushed two fingers inside her tight, hot hole. She lost her mind as the pleasure swamped her. The hard bundle of nerves pulsed as he sucked on it, drawing her closer to her release. He seemed to worship her flesh, licking and sucking while his fingered stroked in and out of her with a steady rhythm. The power he had over her was amazing. Her brain was usually a constant haze of information, but when Sully touched her, there was nothing but him.

Nothing but them.

The tremors began in her belly, muscles tightening, then seemed to shatter out as she climaxed. She felt him slide lower so he could push his tongue deep, collecting her release and drinking it down as the waves of ecstasy rolled through her. It felt like she had shattered into a million tiny pieces, and the only thing holding her together was him.

Archer let out a low growl as the taste of her exploded on his tongue. She was the perfect combination of sweet and salty, and the flavor of her just made him want more. His hands moved to her thighs, holding her open as her body bucked against him. He wanted her to scream his name, to tell him that she was his. He needed her as desperate for him as he was for her, and he damn well

64

wouldn't stop until he got what he wanted. The sounds of her moans were like the sweetest music, making him determined to drive her up again.

"Sully!"

Her back bowed and arched as she came again, this time her entire body shook as the shockwaves pulsed through her. Not giving her any time to recover, he moved over her, pushing her thighs wider. His cock was a steel-hard spike, and with one hard shove, he surged inside of her, sliding deep so they were one.

"You okay?" he asked, his breath coming in pants.

"Better than okay. I can feel you throbbing inside of me. Sully, I never knew…"

He groaned as he saw the tears sparkling in her eyes. He leaned down and captured her lips with his, kissing her lightly as he fought to hold himself still. "Please don't cry, hummingbird."

"It's so right. It feels so right to be with you like this," she whispered, eyes bright with emotion. "Make love with me, Sully. Make me yours."

"You are mine," he whispered as he pulled out, then surged forward, shoving the entire length of his cock deep inside her again. He captured her passionate scream with his mouth, stroking his tongue deep as he began to move inside her.

Serra's legs lifted, one to wrap around his waist while the other hooked behind his knee. She wanted them skin to skin, to feel his corded muscles against her as he drove inside her over and over again. This was a claiming. Of body and soul. Her hips lifted, meeting his every thrust and her fingers dug into his back, holding on as they moved together.

"My sweet, sweet, Serra. You are so fucking beautiful."

"More. Give me more, Sully."

The sound of her plea had need taking over.

Archer braced his knees on the bed so he could pound inside of her tight, hot pussy. His mouth trailed down her throat, teeth nipping lightly across her neck. He could feel the frantic beat of her

65

pulse under her skin, and it thrilled him. White hot pleasure surged through his body each time he drove into her. The feel of her body welcoming him set his own on fire. When her head fell to the side and her eyes closed, it had him snarling.

"Open your eyes, damn you. Open your eyes and look at me."

Her eyes popped back open in shock as one of his large hands moved under her ass, lifting her up to meet him as he hammered into her with a hard, punishing rhythm.

"Tell me again. Tell me your mine."

"I'm yours," she swore. "I always have been."

He let out a low growl as he claimed her mouth again, pushing his tongue deep as he forced both of them toward release. Shifting slightly to his side, he used one hand to reach between them so he could rub her clit. He was damn close, but he needed to make her come again before he let himself take the fall.

"Sully!"

Her body bucked beneath him as the pleasure erupted inside of her. The tight grip of her pussy was too much for him as it fluttered around his cock, taking him with her over the edge. He slammed his cock deep, grinding his hips against her as his hot seed shot out of the head of his cock, filling her completely.

Archer collapsed, careful to shift to the side at the last second so his full weight wasn't on her, but he kept his dick inside her tight sheath, unable to bear being parted from her yet. He nuzzled his head against her, rubbing his nose against her cheek in an affectionate gesture that seemed almost more intimate than the sex had been. Not that the sex wasn't mind blowing. When he had come inside of her, he'd felt like he was giving her a part of his soul.

This was what he had been waiting for his whole life.

To feel connected, and wanted...and whole.

"Sully?"

"Yeah?"

"You can totally get rid of my vibrator."

He snorted out a laugh as he raised himself up on an elbow. "Is that right?"

She nodded solemnly. "Yes. I'll even give you my back-up."

"You have a back-up?"

"Of course I do. Wow, that was… Is sex always like that?"

His eyes narrowed. "You have that look in your eye, and I don't like it."

"What look?"

"The look that says you are calculating something in your head. Forget it, hummingbird. The only men that will ever be in your bed are me and Jax. There will be no comparisons or experimenting with any other men."

Rolling her eyes, she pushed at his sweaty chest. "Of course not, you fool. I haven't avoided men all my life just to go bed hopping. Besides, I'm a claimed woman now."

"Damn right you are." He loved that she could even look haughty buck naked, with her hair all disheveled and spread out over the pillow. Archer leaned down and brushed his lips against hers, then laughed as her stomach rumbled. "I think we need to feed you."

"I think you're right," she said with a smile. "Then after, I think we might need to do a little more experimenting."

The little hellion looked pretty satisfied with herself as his cock twitched and rapidly began to grow inside her pussy again. "Eat fast."

Chapter Five

Serra cut through the cool, blue water, loving the peaceful feeling she always got when she was swimming.

It was late in the evening, and she'd been thrilled when Sully told her they had a full length pool in the lower level of the residence. After they'd eaten and had another bout of love play, she'd decided to make use of the pool so she could clear her head. Sully let her have her quiet time, knowing that she often needed to be by herself when she was trying to assimilate too many emotions at once.

It was amazing having two men that understood her so well, despite the time they had spent apart. Serra used the time in the pool to try to figure out the issue of someone trying to sell the stealth technology she had created. The first person that came to mind was her mother, however there were several reasons why Serra rejected her as a viable suspect. For one, Tania Lysander-Dobbs was a tech-idiot. She may have been able to hire someone to put a block on Serra's transmissions, but her mother could barely handle her own wrist unit to make calls, let alone figure out how the stealth tech worked well enough to try to sell it.

The other main reason that it couldn't have been Tania was she was way too selfish to put something like this together. It would take time and energy away from her spa treatments and many affairs to arrange for the sale of something this intricate. There would have to be tests and meetings, not to mention access to the black market.

Serra knew about the various lovers her mother had taken over the years, and it stung even more knowing that Tania had tried to condemn her to a life alone. The thought that her mother had connections to the Tarin was disturbing, even more so that she had been able to keep their horrible trip to Tartarus all those years ago off the visitor's logs. Still, there was a level of skill that was needed for a sale of this magnitude, and it just didn't fit.

Now that Serra knew of the potential problem, she could take steps to figure out who was involved with the plot and how to stop it. She thought over several different ideas that she wanted to discuss with Jax and Sully as she finished her last lap in the pool. Surfacing, she saw something out of the corner of her eye, and turned her head to see Jax sitting on one of the recliners, watching her with that intense stare of his that always made her insides quiver.

"You always did swim like a fish."

"Pervert."

A wicked grin spread over his devastatingly handsome face. "It's not my fault you're swimming naked, however I do have to say I'm really enjoying the view. I've imagined seeing you like this a million times, but nothing can compare to the real thing. If you think me watching you is perverted, just wait until I get my hands on you."

His words had a thrill of anticipation shooting through her blood stream, making her tingle in all the right places. Treading water over to the side of the pool, she laid her arms on the edge, stationing herself as she drank in the sight of him. They stared at each other in silence, their eyes conveying a million emotions that no words would ever be accurate enough to express.

"Thank you, Jax."

His expression sobered, and a dark glint sparked to life in his grey eyes that seemed to see everything. "I don't think you understand how this all works, Serra. There is *nothing* I wouldn't do for you. Do you hear me? Nothing. You don't need to thank me. Ever."

It was baffling to her, but she was beginning to understand the depth and scope of their feelings for her. And wasn't that miraculous? She had never thought to have anyone in her life that she could depend on, who would put her first. But now she had two, powerful men that would always keep her safe. Her feelings for them had always been strong, but now, being claimed by them had made her love them even more.

It might have been strange to anyone else since they had spent so much time away from one another, but Serra knew that didn't matter. She had given her heart to Jax and Sully when she was but a girl, and now, she loved them as a woman. Once her heart had been given, there was never any other choice for her.

They were hers just as she belonged to them.

Forever.

"Did your interrogation prove satisfactory this afternoon?"

Jax nodded. "I supervised while Dom and Arik interrogated both of your guards. We are confident they have nothing to do with the potential theft."

"Good. I like Officer Meyer and Officer Rhine."

"How much do you like them?" he asked darkly.

She rolled her eyes at him. "Shut down your thrusters, Commander. I'm aware that my guards are your men, and I'm sure you gave them all kinds of inventive threats when you had them assigned to me. Since they've always been highly respectful and never once caused me any trouble, I would have to say they are very loyal to you."

His lips twitched as he fought back a smile. "How did you know?"

"I know you, but Sully confirmed it. Oh, and I'd like my necklace back that they took off me in medical." She smirked at him. "Even though you know where I am now, I'm still attached to it, and would like it back."

Surprise had his eyes widening. "You knew about the tracker?"

Men. Seriously, her bonded needed to learn a thing or two…

"Of course I did. Just as I knew as soon as I reported that guard you would have him replaced." She laughed as Jax frowned as if he didn't like that she had figured it all out. "Jax, there was no way you guys were going to stop worrying about me. Even when I stopped hearing from you, I knew that I could count on you if I needed you."

Jax's expression turned absolutely lethal. "We didn't know you were trying to contact us."

"I know." Not wanting to dwell on that, she changed the subject. "But you claimed me."

Satisfaction gleamed in his eyes, turning them so bright they shone like two silver stars. "Yes, we claimed you."

"You sound very pleased with yourself."

"I am. I'm also very pleased with you. There has never been anyone else for me or Archer. You've been ours since we were young. You know it's true."

"I'm not denying it. I assume Sully told you what happened this afternoon?" She tried to keep her voice neutral, but could feel the heat spread across her cheeks, belying her calm.

"Oh yeah," he growled. "Did he make your first time good for you, sweetheart?"

Good? That was a grossly inaccurate description for what she and Sully had shared together. "It was better than good. Thank you for giving me time to acclimate to having two lovers. I know it must have been difficult for you to wait."

"Sweetheart, I've waited years for you, a few hours more didn't kill me. Although, it feels like it might now that I've seen you naked." He took a deep breath, then let it out slowly. "We didn't want to overwhelm you with our attentions. How do you feel about having two lovers now?"

"I was always meant to be with you and Sully. I truly believe that," she whispered. "The thought of having both of you…it's highly arousing."

There was an intensity in his gaze now that made her so hot, she was surprised the water around her wasn't boiling. Her eyes widened he took off his boots, one at a time, then he stood up and slowly began to undress. "What are you doing?"

He continued to stare at her as he tossed his uniform jacket onto the recliner, then quickly pulled off his shirt, baring his impressive chest. "I thought I would join you…for a swim."

Where Sully was slightly taller than Jax at six-foot-eight, with a leaner frame, Jax was thicker with heavy muscles in his arms and chest. It was a chest that Serra desperately wanted to touch, to feel the muscles tense under her fingertip as she stroked her hand down the contours of his hard abs. He seemed to watch her as if searching for a sign of unease, but she was done holding back her desire for him.

She was done holding anything back.

Quirking a brow at him, she lazily trailed a finger on the edge of the pool. "Is that all you want to do? Swim? I had another activity in mind…"

Jax's hands paused in the middle of unfastening his pants. He wanted to curse as his cock pulsed in anticipation. "What did you have in mind, sweetheart?"

She moved down the length of the pool until she was able to stand. "I want you right here," she said patting the edge. "Earlier with Sully, I didn't really get to see him. I was hoping…you'd let me look at you."

"Serra, you can look at me all you want." His lips curved up in a tender smile even as his eyes heated to molten silver. "Sweetheart, I know you need to study everything. This wouldn't be any different."

"I've always been fascinated by the male form, but I've never really gotten to look at one up close."

"You better not have," he growled.

She couldn't help but smirk at him. "Settle down, Commander. Do I have to remind you that the first man I've ever been with was Sully? It's not like you and he haven't had your share of women over these last few years."

"I don't think this is something we should be talking about right now."

Amusement flittered through her as she watched him squirm. Laughter bubbled up. "Is the great Jax Spartan, Commander of the Capital, actually embarrassed?"

"Shut up."

She laughed again. "Honestly, I know you've been with other women in the past. I'm pragmatic, not stupid. It's only logical. As long your body belongs to me now, I don't care what happened before you claimed me." She sobered as a distressing thought entered her mind. "You don't plan on being with anyone else, do you?"

"What? No! Good God, woman. What do you take me for? I wouldn't have claimed you if I wanted to be with anyone else. Now that you're mine, I have no need for any other woman."

She nearly slumped in relief. "I had to ask. After seeing the way my fathers have taken mistresses over the years, and the way my mother flaunts her lovers...I just needed to know."

"I understand, but you don't have to worry about that. Sully and I would never cheat on you. I can promise you we'll keep you so busy, none of us would even have time to think about anyone else. You're who I want. You always have been. Just thinking about touching you makes me hard." Jax quickly removed his pants so he was standing completely nude.

Serra sucked in a harsh breath as she admired his strong, beautiful body. He was like sculpted marble, all hard muscle and sinew covered with golden flesh. She loved the hard contours of his body, and the large cock that jutted out proudly from between his thighs.

She was fascinated by the differences between their bodies, and wanted to look at him, up close and personal. He reminded her of a large jungle cat, and she was mesmerized by the way his muscles moved as he stalked forward. Lust mixed with curiosity when he sat down right in front of her. She drank him in, studying the rigid shaft that had filled and risen so it slapped against his hard abs.

Positioning herself between his legs, she hesitated before she set her hands down on his hard thighs. The solid muscle beneath her fingers flexed as she slid her hands up slowly. Tearing her gaze away from his straining flesh, she looked up into his eyes, needing to ask him for what she wanted. As if he knew she was holding back, he frowned at her.

"What do you want, Serra? Ask me and it's yours."

"I…I want to study you. Is that bad?"

"Go ahead, baby. But I have to warn you, I'm already riding the edge. It won't take much to push me over. I want you too much, and having you stare at my dick isn't helping."

She looked back down at his hard flesh and saw his shaft jerk under her gaze. "It seems to like the attention," she murmured.

He choked back a laugh. "You are going to be the death of me, woman."

She glanced back up at him and smiled, knowing he could see the emotions swirling in her eyes. "No, Jax. I'm going to be your life, as you will be mine."

"Serra," Jax growled low in his throat. "Finish your inspection before I take you right here on the damn floor."

Hearing the strain in his voice, she decided to stop stalling and get on with her experiment. She knew he was holding onto his control by a thin thread from the tension all but radiating from him. Looking at him like this was an experience unlike any other she'd ever had. She wasn't just a scientist studying a subject. She was a woman learning her lover's body.

Serra had often heard other women talking about their sex partners. She'd heard men's penises often described as being odd looking, or even strange and ugly. Now, seeing Jax with her own eyes, Serra knew they were wrong.

Jax was beautiful…every single inch of him.

His hard cock was large and thick, with heavy veins pulsing under the skin of the shaft. The mushroomed head looked soft, almost supple, and she was utterly enthralled as a drop of liquid appeared at the tip from the tiny hole at the end. Pre-cum. She knew what it was, but had never seen it before.

And she wanted to taste it…taste him.

Jax leaned back on his hands, letting his head fall back as he let her do her thing. It was a kind of torture. To sit there patiently and let her study him, when all he wanted to do was throw her on the ground and pound himself into her until he got rid of the damn hard-on he'd been packing for days. He knew about her need to understand everything around her, and he struggled to give her that. Jax not only wanted her to be comfortable with his body, he also wanted her to be able to ask him for anything she needed.

It had been difficult for him to leave her earlier, allowing her time with Archer so she wouldn't feel overwhelmed or unsure about their commitment to caring for her. He'd seen too many other bonding units run into issues if both men claimed a woman together the first time they introduced her to the pleasures they could give her, and he didn't want that for Serra. Stepping back had been hard as hell, but he hadn't been lying when he said he would do anything for her.

Shit, he'd kill for her…waiting a few hours to fuck the hell out of her wasn't even in his top ten list of difficult tasks he'd do for her. He let his mind drift as he closed his eyes, trying to relax, but they popped back open as he let out a hoarse shout when he felt her tongue lap at the pre-cum dripping from the head of his cock.

Holy galactic sonic boom, she really was trying to fucking kill him!

Serra hummed in her throat as the taste of him exploded on her tongue. His flavor was rich, almost earthy, salty with a hint of sweetness she hadn't expected. She was encouraged by his throaty growl, and engulfed the head of his cock into her mouth, sucking lightly on the spongy head as she swirled her tongue around it to collect another pulse of pre-cum.

"Sweet God, baby! Fuck, that's good. Suck it. Suck my cock for me."

She lifted her lashes, and her body went hot as she saw the primal need shining from his eyes. His hips jerked as she reached up and squeezed his cock with her hand, pulling the rigid shaft down so she could get a better angle. He was enormous. Long and thick, and her fingers didn't meet as they wrapped around him. She loved the dichotomy of sucking on the soft head while holding the hard length of him in her hand.

Moving her hand, she felt his skin slide a little as she pumped it over his straining shaft. She took more of him into her mouth, careful not to scrape her teeth along the sensitive flesh of his cock while she sucked him. Using her other hand to brace herself, her nails dug into his thigh as he fisted her hair. There was just enough bite when he pulled at the long locks to add to her own pleasure as she went to work.

"Fuck! Serra, your hot, little mouth feels like heaven."

Jax used every ounce of willpower within him to keep from spilling as soon as she'd taken his cock into her mouth. He swore viciously as she took his cock to the back of her throat. What she lacked in experience, she sure as hell made up for with enthusiasm. White-hot heat shot through his system as he watched her suck his cock. His body jerked again as if shocked by a laser blast when she swirled her tongue underneath the tip of the head, stroking over sensitive flesh.

"God damn it, I'm close, sweetheart. Pull back if you don't want me to shoot my cum down your throat," he cautioned, but she just kept going. He felt her moan vibrate down his shaft as she took him back to her throat, and he let out another curse as she moved her hand from his thigh to cup his balls.

"You want it? You're gonna get it. Suck me, baby."

He took control, damning himself as he did. He'd let her play, but he couldn't stand it any longer. Tightening his hold on her wet hair, he guided her head over him, stroking his cock into her mouth faster. She moaned again as she sucked him into the hot the recesses of her mouth.

"I'm coming, Serra. Drink me down," he commanded.

With a harsh grunt, he came. He watched with awe as she eagerly took what he fed her, drinking down his hot semen as he spurted down her throat. She swallowed each pulse of his seed, not letting go of him until she milked him dry.

Serra pulled back, but before she could even catch her breath, Jax pushed to his feet. He squatted down, curling his hands under her arms, lifting her out of the pool so the water fell off her in sheets.

"Jax! What—?" Her question was cut off as he quickly carried her over to a lounge chair and dropped her down onto it.

"My turn. Come here, I wanna eat that sweet pussy." Parting her thighs so he could kneel between them, Jax lifted her legs and draped over his shoulders. She let out a scream as his hot tongue pushed inside her pussy, lapping at her cream that was mixed with the water from the pool. He worked her ruthlessly to a fast, hard climax that had her gripping the edges of the lounge chair, desperate for something to hold on to.

She was still shuddering when Jax straightened, sliding her body to the edge of the chair as he held her thighs open. With one quick thrust his cock pierced her body, filling her pussy full.

"Jax!"

"You okay, baby?"

"Yes, but good God. Give a girl some notice, would you?"

Jax grinned down at her as he leaned forward to press a kiss to her lips. He pushed his tongue deep, stroking inside her mouth and felt her arms come up to wind around his neck. He tasted himself on her, and he shared her own essence back to her. Some men got weirded out by the idea of kissing a woman after she went down on them, but not him. If Serra was willing to drink his seed down, then he sure as hell wasn't going to mind kissing her after. Nothing they did together was wrong. Nothing was off limits.

"Your enhancements are impressive," she murmured against his lips, making him laugh.

"Same goes, sweetheart." He began to move inside her, thrusting in and out of her pussy with strong, sure strokes. He loved the way she welcomed him, never once hesitating to meet him beat for beat as she lifted her hips.

"How can you still be hard? You just came."

"Serra, I have waited years for you. I think I'm going to stay hard whenever you're around for quite a while." Cutting off whatever she was going to say, he took her lips again in a scorching kiss. Hell, he could keep kissing her forever. He ran his hands over her body, touching every inch of her that he could reach. Tongues danced together as he fucked her slowly, their bodies rocking in concert.

He wanted to love her gently, to show her how much he had missed her all the years they had spent apart, but a raw hunger was taking over, stealing his senses. He needed her...so much he felt like he would die if he didn't come inside her soon.

Riding the dark lust burning inside of him, Jax pulled out of her, flipping her body over on the lounge chair so she was kneeling in front of him. She let out a startled yelp that changed to a moan when he shoved his cock back inside her.

"I can go deeper this way," he told her, whispering in her ear as he cupped her breasts, pinching lightly at her nipples. "Do you feel that? Can you feel your snug, little pussy gripping my cock?"

"God, yes. It feels so good."

Serra moaned again as he covered her body with his, pushing her down so her upper body was flat against the chair while his knees forced hers wider. She felt him filling her, loving the slide of his hard cock inside her wet heat. Overwhelmed by the pleasure he gave her, she closed her eyes, letting him drive her closer toward the ecstasy she knew waited.

But it stayed right out of reach.

"Jax. I need..."

Knowing exactly what he was doing to her, Jax bit down lightly on the skin of her shoulder before soothing the sting with his tongue. "Tell me what you need, Serra. Use your words. Ask me and I'll give you anything...everything. Do you need me to pound my cock into your tight, little cunt to get you off? Is that what you want? Or do you need me to rub your clit while I take you? Tell me."

"Stars, the way you talk to me..."

"It turns you on, admit it," Jax demanded. "I can feel your cream soaking my cock. You will learn to crave feeling me inside you like this, just as much as I do. You're my chosen, my claimed, and I'm your bonded. You need to tell me what you need so I can give it to you."

"I need more, Jax. Give me more. Give me all you got. Don't you dare hold back on me!"

Jax let out a low growl as he did exactly as she asked. Letting go of the last strains of his control, he powered into her from behind. His cock hammered into her pussy with hard, fast strokes, making her scream out in pleasure. Wrapping his arms around her chest, he held her tight to him, practically surrounding her with his body as he drove them both closer to release.

"Come, Serra. Come and take me with you. Do it!"

She cried out his name as she came, her pussy squeezing down so hard on his shaft that he could barely move. He forced his way past her tight pussy muscles once, twice more, then spilled himself deep inside her.

He collapsed onto her, using his arms to brace some of his weight so she wasn't crushed beneath him. "You're mine, baby," he whispered against her ear, then kissed her neck.

He felt her lips curve against his arm. "And you are all mine, Commander."

"Forever."

She let out a wheezing laugh. "That is, if you and Sully don't kill me with sex first."

Jax turned her head to rub his lips lightly against hers. "True. But it would be a hell of a way to go."

Chapter Six

"Mmm, this is real coffee."

Serra all but purred as she took another sip of the rich, dark brew. It was morning, and she sat in the sunroom right off the living room, more content than she'd felt in a very long time. It was a little chilly outside, but the full glass windows allowed for the sun to kiss her skin with warmth.

"Nothing but the best for our woman." Jax leaned back in his chair, watching her with a look of smug satisfaction she thought she would have to get used to.

He had been looking at her like that ever since they'd woken up.

After she and Jax had left the pool area, they had eaten a quick meal, then they had taken a long, hot shower, where he had introduced her to the pleasure of bathing together. She had loved rubbing her soapy hands over his golden skin, but she loved what he did to her with his strong, rough hands even more. Jax loved her with an intensity that stole her breath every time he touched her. He was dominant, yet gentle. Kind, yet ruthless with the way he played her body until she was close to begging for release.

Sully had come back from the office just as they had been settling into bed for the night. It was a heady feeling to have two men want her so much that they couldn't keep their hands off of her. She had wanted to be with both of them, but she was too exhausted and could barely keep her eyes open long enough to say good night. They had been extremely understanding, tucking her between them so she could sleep sheltered between their large, warm bodies, with her half-draped over Sully while Jax spooned her from behind.

She'd always wondered what it would be like to spoon with someone. To have their body pressed tight against hers. In the past when she'd thought about it, the concept had left her feeling panicked. She knew that was partly because of whatever programming her mother had done to her, but another part had been due to her dislike of being touched.

It was different with Jax and Sully.

Feeling them surrounding her had been better than any blanket, and the close contact of their bodies comforted her in a way she had never thought possible. She'd gone to sleep with a smile on her face, and had woken up the same way.

Serra had wanted to get frisky with them, but there hadn't been time since they were going to have company shortly. They'd had just enough time to get dressed, then they'd headed downstairs to wait for Arik and Dom to join them for breakfast.

She liked seeing them like this, relaxed and at ease, since it so rarely happened. Even when they were young, they had only been like this when they had been alone. Both men looked handsome in plain black shirts and drawstring pants. She was dressed in similar fashion, but had chosen to wear a pale-green color that matched her eyes.

Serra took another sip of her coffee, then frowned down into her cup. Her lashes fluttered in surprise when Sully ran a finger lightly over the crease in her brow.

"I don't like seeing you frown, baby."

She smiled at him as she leaned into the large hand that cupped her cheek. "Sorry, I was just thinking."

"About?" he prompted.

"I know that Arik and Dominic are your friends, but I find something…unsettling about Dominic."

"I'm not surprised," Jax said so matter-of-factly, it startled her. "Dominic Stryker is a good man, but he can be intimidating."

"Says the commander who strikes fear into the hearts of all."

He grinned at her. "You don't fear me."

"That's because you've never turned the wrath of Jax on me."

Jax's smile turned to a frown as he glared at Archer, who simply laughed. "Do you know how annoying that is?"

82

Archer sent him a droll stare. "Live with it."

Jax ignored his best friend and turned back to her. "Anyways, I think Dom makes you uncomfortable because he's part Tarin."

Her eyes widened. "But he's human!"

"He is, but one of his ancestors was Tarin," Archer explained. "During the war with Earth, Dom's great, great-grandfather or whatever saved a Tarin woman and took her as his consort when he ended up falling in love with her. A consort is like their version of a claiming."

That brought a smile to her face. It was nice to hear that the couple had found love after suffering the pain of war. Centuries ago, when Earth had gone to war with the Tarin, many of the female Tarin took the opportunity to flee due to their having little more than slave status on their home world. Many things had changed over the years, but it was still a struggle that led to Tartarus engaging in a civil war that was still being fought.

Serra nodded. "Just thinking about the Tarin makes me unsettled."

Sully reached out and stroked a hand over her arm. "After what was done to you, I'd be surprised if you didn't feel that way."

"Having your mind fucked with that way would put anyone off," Jax added.

She blew out a slow breath, pleased that they seemed to understand. "But he's your friend, so I'm sure I will like him once I get to know him. Can you tell me a little bit about him? I know Arik through the mind scan he did on me, but Dom is still an unknown entity."

"The men in Dom's family have been part of Earth's military service, dating back all the way to the early twenty-first century," Jax explained. "There aren't many men, if any, that I trust as completely as Archer, but I would trust Dom with my life. Even more important, I would trust him with yours."

That was all she needed to hear. "Okay. If you trust them, then so will I. Until or unless he does something to disprove that confidence."

"That's all we can ask for," Jax agreed with a smile.

Archer stood up and programmed the food console to replicate various items for their breakfast, and came back to the table carrying multiple platters of food. "You think this will be enough?"

"Are you kidding? That's enough to feed an entire unit in space for a month!" Serra gasped.

Jax shrugged. "If we need more we can program it."

She shook her head. "I'm surprised you don't have helpers here in your home, either human or android."

"It's your home now, too," Jax reminded her. He waited for her to nod in agreement before he explained. "We have a few droids, but we rarely use them. We also have enough assistants following us around all damn day that we don't want anyone around when we're at home."

"That makes sense. I was just curious. As you know, I don't like having too many people around to function at full capacity myself."

"We know, hummingbird," Archer said as he sat back down, then he leaned in to brush his lips against hers before settling back in his chair. "We'll do whatever it is you need to make you comfortable in our home."

"Thank you."

"Stop thanking us," Jax snapped, making her laugh at the irritation in his voice.

"So," Serra began as she set her cup back down on the table. "After this meeting is over I want to go in and get my birth control deactivated."

Sully sputtered as he choked on the coffee he'd just taken a sip of. "Damn it, woman. Give a man some warning, would you?"

"Is that something you'd like me to wait to have done? Is it too soon?"

84

"No, sweetheart. I think it's a fantastic idea," Jax whispered as he reached out and stroked a hand over her hair. Just the thought of seeing Serra swell with their child had him going hard as stone, making him shift in his chair to alleviate the pressure of his pants pushing against his straining shaft.

"It's been something that I've been thinking about for quite a while now. I've always wanted to have children. I believe I would be a good mother, and I think with our genetics, we would make an exceptional child." She lost her smile for a moment, and an almost desperate look filled her eyes. "I won't be like my mother. I know I can be too analytical, and I'm not—"

"Stop. Serra, I don't ever want to hear you saying something like that again. You are perfect just the way you are. You would make a wonderful mother. You *will* be a wonderful mother," Jax said with fervor. "I thought we'd have to wait until you were more at ease with us, but I'm ready if you are. We can take you to medical right after our meeting."

She beamed at him, and ran her foot up his leg under the table until it stroked over his cock. "Hmm...now I can't wait to get started trying."

Jax jerked her head forward and took her lips in a heated kiss. Passion flared to life as their tongues dueled together. He couldn't get enough of her. Her taste, her scent, everything about her aroused him to the point of pain.

"Damn it, now I'm hard as hell, and I can't do anything about it," Archer muttered as the door chime sounded, announcing that their visitors had arrived.

Jax released Serra and she sat back in her chair with a sigh that instantly changed to a yelp as Archer plucked her out of her seat and settled her on his lap. "You can't kiss Jax like that and not give me some loving, too."

She smiled at him and wound her arms around his neck. "We can't have that now, can we?"

She kissed him as Jax checked the outside monitor to make sure it was Dom and Arik at their door. He let them in by imputing a code into the tablet on the table, then called out to their guests to inform them where they were.

When Dom and Arik walked into the room, Dom immediately scowled. "Damn it. Do we need to leave?"

Archer chuckled as he helped Serra back into her own seat. "Calm down. It's nothing you haven't seen before."

After greetings were exchanged, Dom and Arik took their seats and all the men immediately started filling their plates with food. Serra looked up as Sully set a special plate in front of her filled with a variety of offerings. It was white just like the rest of the plates, but this one had slightly raised partitions on it, so each item of food was in its own little compartment. He winked at her. "I know you don't like for your food to touch," he whispered after he sat back down.

It moved her that both he and Jax did so many little things they knew would make her feel more comfortable. Because her brain didn't function like most, she had come to learn to accept that she was different, but people still though she was weird. Sully and Jax knew her idiosyncrasies, and still cared for her. In fact, they somehow saw her differences as something that made her special…in a good way.

How amazing was that?

As they began to eat, she took a moment to center her thoughts by taking a sip of coffee before she addressed the group. "I know that you're here to discuss the issue of someone trying to steal the stealth tech that I've created. Since we all know it isn't me, I'm assuming the goal would be to track down who is really planning this potential sale?"

"I'd say that is accurate," Arik agreed.

She smiled at the handsome D'Aire male, then had to stop from rolling her eyes as Jax bristled next to her. "Since that is the next step, I'd like to share a plan I've come up with. Since learning about this disturbing scenario, I've been trying to figure out who would be involved in this, but I just don't know of anyone who would do such a thing."

"It's not your fault, Serra," Archer said, putting his hand on her arm. "There is no way you could have known this was happening."

"Someone who is willing to sell our tech on the black market would be good with hiding their identity," Dom added, darkly. "He or she wouldn't give a shit—sorry, I mean they wouldn't care what rules they had to break to get the deal done."

Jax filled her cup with more steaming coffee. "Don't worry. You're clear of this, sweetheart. We'll catch whoever is behind this, and make sure they pay." He turned to Dom. "You guys have eyes on Serra's other guards and her mother?"

"We do."

"Well, that's what I wanted to talk to you about. I don't think my mother had anything to do with this. That's not emotion talking. She just isn't capable." She laid out her reasoning for them, and got a nod from Arik.

"I agree. From your memories of your mother, she does not seem a likely suspect. She is more than capable of doing all kinds of immoral activities to ensure she is able to live in the style of which she has become accustomed. However, her time is spent on selfish endeavors that would not allow her to put something like this together."

"You may be right, but we still have to keep her under surveillance until we figure out who is controlling the sale. She could be working with someone," Archer ordered, then winced as he looked back at Serra. "Sorry, hummingbird."

"It's all right. Nothing she does would surprise me now."

He lifted her hand to press a kiss to her palm before addressing the rest of the table. "But the question is, are they after the finalized schematics or the actual prototype for the stealth tech?"

"The prototype is being tested on the base right outside of Light City. Serra wouldn't be authorized to take it off the premises," Jax replied. "But what I don't get is if someone had a backdoor into her data unit, why not just steal the specs before now? Why wait?"

"Because they couldn't," Serra said softly. "All of my notes and schematics are in code."

"Explain," Jax demanded.

She shot him a frown at his barked command. "When I'm working on an experiment, it is easier for me to work in a sort of shorthand. It allows me to recalculate without backtracking as much. I started using it when I was a teenager, since I was tired of the older scientists stealing my work."

"Did that happen often? People stealing your work?" Archer asked, sounding outraged.

She nibbled at her lip before answering. "Yes and no. When I was young, many of my instructors would study my work to try and disprove it. Sometimes they ended up using it as a springboard for something they were working on, while other times I was put on a team to help with something they were stuck on."

"That must have been frustrating for you," Arik said with a kind smile. "Being more intelligent than your trainers would not have made for a comfortable work environment."

"It wasn't. It didn't bother me that I didn't get credit for what I helped them with, but I had my own projects I wanted to work on. And when I refused to do their work because I wanted to work on my own, it was difficult, but I got clearance so there was nothing they could do." Her eyes widened as she looked at her bonded. "Did you—"

"We can't take credit for that one," Archer said around a mouthful of food. "Regent Spartan took care of that for you."

She smiled at them, knowing the regent would have never thought to do it if her men hadn't asked. "What was I saying? Oh, yes. Once I began working on my own projects I just adapted the code since it's what I'm used to. The only other person that can understand it is my main assistant. It took him years to learn it, and he still has issues at times. That's why whoever is after the tech needs to wait."

"I still don't get it," Dom said. "Dumb it down for us, Serra."

Excitement bubbled inside her as things began to fall in place. "Don't you see? Once I was ready to bring the concept to the Alliance, I transferred the specs on site for the team in Light City. Whoever is after the tech didn't understand my code and couldn't break into their system, so they had to wait until after the prototype was created and the final tests are run. They have to be waiting for me to be given the finalized schematics, which I will once we calibrate the prototype for anything we find during testing. That's what they're waiting for, I know it is."

"So, why don't we just destroy the link on the data unit?" Arik suggested.

"Or postpone the testing until we catch these fuckers." Dom amended.

Serra shook her head. "We can't do that."

"We can," Archer countered. "You're clear of this and we want you to stay that way. I'll be damned if someone is going to try to use you to commit treason. And they were. Whoever is behind this was setting you up to take the fall."

"And when I find the son of a bitch behind this, I'm going to make him wish he decided to boot his own ass out of an air lock in space instead of dealing with me." The threat was said in a voice so filled with rage that Serra had no doubt Jax was serious.

"Now, this is going to be fun," Dom said, his dark eyes glittering with anticipation as he refilled his plate with food. "It's been a while since I've gotten down and dirty with you, Jax. Arik here is of a more peaceful nature."

"Logical. You mean logical. You can't just go around killing suspects. If they're guilty—"

"They signed their own termination orders as soon as they got involved with this," Archer argued. "We'll get the information we need first. We always do."

The smile on the men's faces sent a shiver down Serra's spine. "I think I've come up with a plan that will help us catch whoever is behind this without beating confessions out of people."

"You aren't getting anywhere near these assholes, Serra," Jax ordered harshly.

"Listen," she said in a rush, wanting to pitch her idea before he argued anymore. "While I was swimming yesterday I figured out how to build a track and trace program that will stop the data flow to the outside source on an outgoing relay basis. We can use it to filter whatever information we want, like faulty schematics so that they will think they have the finalized plans, but I can ensure it won't work. If those plans are transferred, we can tag it with a digital marker that will lead us straight to the buyer, but this will only work if the tests are completed as scheduled. If you pull me out now, they'll know we're on to them."

She waited for a response, but was only met with silence. Looking around, she saw that all of the men were gawking at her. Sully and Dom's hands were frozen in mid-air, their forks halfway to their mouths. Arik had a small smile on his face, while Jax simply stared at her. "What?"

"How long was your swim?" Dom asked incredulously.

"About a half an hour, give or take a few minutes."

Archer smirked at Dom. "Our woman is wicked smart."

Serra preened a little bit from his compliment, but tried to hide it. "Thank you. You know this is a better plan, and it will allow us to follow the seller back to whoever their contacts are on the other end. In order to create the program, I'll need access to a lab with better equipment then you have here. Speaking of, you know none of this would have happened if I'd been allowed to build my own data unit instead of using the Alliance crap they give everyone."

"Let it go, baby," Archer said, patting her knee.

She glared at him. "I need my assistant, too."

"No."

"Non-negotiable, Jax. I need Troy Takeshi to do this." She held up a hand. "Don't even start with me. I know he works for you, too. If you didn't trust him, you would never have assigned him to me four years ago."

Jax let out a weary sigh. "How did you know?"

"Maybe it was the way he never once looked at me as more than a colleague, or maybe it could have been how he turned into a freaking ninja every time someone bothered me. Science geeks usually aren't trained to know a hundred ways to kill someone with a coffee cup."

Archer, Dom and Arik laughed, but Jax glared at her, not amused. "Who exactly was bothering you and why didn't I hear about this?"

She rolled her eyes. "Probably because the situations were taken care of, and it was nothing for you to be worried about. Like last month for instance, when we were on our way to The Black Hole on Alpha Station: X2 when those—"

Archer lost his smile "You went where?"

"What the hell were your guards thinking letting you go there? The Krytos who own that bar are fucking crazy!" Jax exploded. "Not to mention all the other scum that take refuge in that sanctuary! And Officer Takeshi was with you? That's it, I'm busting him down to—"

"You will not," Serra ordered. "Besides, it's not his place to tell me where I could go. He was and is my assistant, not my keeper."

"You always were stubborn," Jax muttered.

Serra let out a delicate snort as she speared a fresh berry with her fork. "I am."

"Why were you going to the Black Hole, Serra? That place is too wild for you, and I know you don't like crowds," Archer added.

"I was having lunch with Alexis Tesera-Volis and her four, very large, very skilled dragon warrior mates. X2 may not be the calmest station, but you know as well as I do, once I passed through the doors of The Black Hole, the owners would have never let

91

anything happen to me. I've remained friends with Alexis since we were in the Academy together."

Jax waved her on. "So what happened before you got there?"

"Oh, well...there was a Helios male that grabbed me and wanted to scent me—"

"Son of a bitch!"

"Jax," she chided in a tone that seemed to calm him...marginally. "Troy was with me, as were two of my guards. Before my guards even knew what was happening, Troy had done something to the Helios to get him to release me, and I found myself behind his back without even knowing how I got there."

"You could have been hurt," Dom said. "The Helios seek out companions based on scent and if he wanted to smell you then—"

"I know," she said. "But Troy got me away from him. Before the Helios could retaliate, Alexis and her mates arrived and they poofed the Helios male to the other side of the space station, so I didn't have to worry about him anymore."

Dom blinked. "They...what do you mean they poofed him?"

Surprised, Archer asked, "Didn't you know? Those dragon warriors can use magic."

"But they can poof people? That's just not right." Dom glared. "And now you have me saying poofed, damn it. Can we get back to talking about killing people?"

Serra studied the director her bonded called a close friend, and saw that he was a severe man, with an edge of unhappiness all but clinging to him. "I think you need sex."

Dom sputtered, coughing on the coffee he'd just drank. He gawked at her as the rest of the men tried to hold back their laughter. His astonishment turned into a dark glower. "I have sex."

She shook her head, ignoring the other men. "Then perhaps you need to do it more often. Sex released endorphins into the system that elevates stress and enhances mood."

Dom glanced over at Jax. "Is she for real?"

"What?" Serra said, blinking at the table as the other men lost the fight to hold back their hilarity. "From your gruff demeanor, I believe you would benefit from a steady increase of sexual release to improve your disposition. Factoring in that you are also descended from the Tarin in your familial history, you should know that you might need the additional boost to maintain optimal levels of energy."

"I'm fine. Sex is not an issue," Dom gritted out through clenched teeth.

She gave him a thoughtful glance. "Hmm…perhaps the sex you're having isn't the right kind of intercourse you need then."

"Oh, for the love of…will you guys shut the hell up!"

Archer wiped at the tears in his eyes from laughing so hard. "Stars! I haven't laughed like that in ages. What do you mean, by the right kind, baby? I didn't know there was a wrong kind."

"You need lessons or something, Dom?" Jax asked, trying to keep a straight face.

"Fuck all of you."

"Wish we could help you out, but no thanks," Archer said with another laugh.

Serra frowned at them. "I didn't mean it to be malicious. There have been rumors that the Tarin receive higher levels of energy that sustain them longer if they engage in sexual activity with a partner they are emotionally connected to. That's all."

"This conversation is over."

She wanted to say more, but sensed that she had already overstepped a line of propriety that she rarely recognized. Serra was getting ready to apologize when Jax's wrist unit beeped with an incoming call. He looked down then winced as he saw the readout.

"It's my mother."

"Aren't you going to answer it?"

He shook his head, but sighed as the beeping stopped and Archer's wrist unit immediately started beeping. "Shit."

"She knows."

"We don't know that," Jax snapped.

"The hell we don't. You know she knows. She knows everything," Archer responded. He let out a sigh of relief when his wrist unit stopped beeping, then tensed as the home communications console began beeping. "Shit, you have to answer that. She'll kill us if you don't."

"Hell…" Jax picked up the tablet on the table and hit a button. "Answer, voice only. Block outgoing video."

On the wall monitor, Donna Spartan-Rollins' image popped up on screen, her beautiful face marred by the fierce frown she was wearing. "What in the seven hells is this? Why are you blocking me? Jax? Sullivan?"

"We're in a meeting, Mother." Jax said lightly, then winced as the frown on his mother's face darkened.

"A meeting about what? That business with Serra?"

"How do you know about that?"

Donna waved her hand on screen. "You should know better than to ask that question. Your father is still smarting from the tongue lashing I gave him for consenting to have that poor girl taken into custody. Speaking of, the reason I'm contacting you is because we are throwing you a claiming ceremony this evening at the estate."

"That's very kind of you, Mother, but we're busy and—"

"Jax, I think you owe that sweet woman a proper ceremony after the pitiful way you claimed her. Yes, I know about that, too. And don't think we won't be having words about that later."

Jax winced again, then glowered at Dom as the other man chuckled. Jax's mother raised a brow. "Is that Sullivan laughing? I'll be having words with you as well, Sullivan Archer."

"No, ma'am. I wasn't laughing. That was Dom. Dominic Stryker," Archer informed her, not hesitating to throw his friend under the proverbial freight-shuttle.

"Well, then. Isn't this convenient. Make sure you bring Dominic and Arik with you when you come."

"Oh, well. Ma'am, we—"

Donna quickly cut Dom off with a smile that could only be described as lethal. "Since your mother and fathers will also be in attendance, I would hate to tell them that you disregarded my invitation."

"Shit."

"I heard that," she said with a cheerful laugh. "Anyways, it's all been arranged. Everything will be perfect by the time you arrive. Is Serra there?"

Serra shot Jax a slightly terrified glance. "Umm, yes, ma'am."

Donna's smile softened until Serra could all but feel the acceptance and affection coming through the screen. "Serra, dear. We are so very pleased to welcome you into the family. Thank you for putting up with my sons, and I do consider Sullivan a son, just like we consider you our daughter now."

"Thank you," Serra said, her throat tight with emotion. Both Jax and Sully reached out to take her hands in theirs. "And thank you for throwing us a party. I haven't even thought of it since everything has been happening so quickly."

"Leave everything to me, dear. Jax, Sullivan, I want you to bring Serra here in a few hours. We need time to prep."

"Ma, we—"

"Jax, you really don't want to fight me on this. I will see you in a few hours. Love you." The entire room was left staring at the blank screen as Donna Spartan-Rollins cut communications.

"People fear me all over the damn universe, and yet my mother just fucking rolls right over me," Jax muttered as he scowled at the blank screen.

"You aren't the only one," Dom said in commiseration. "I can make grown men cry in interrogation, but my own mother has the power to make me feel like I'm fucking four years old when she uses that tone on me."

Jax sighed as Archer, Serra and Arik laughed. "Well, I guess we can discuss this more on the way to my parents' estate. Looks like we have a party to attend."

Chapter Seven

The Spartan-Rollins' estate was a huge piece of property located on the outskirts of the Capital, where the hustle and bustle of the city gave way to the lush greenery of the coast.

In this section of the city, the wealthy lived lavishly in a facsimile of the years on Earth before the Alien Wars. The shuttle touched down onto the ground right outside of the electric gate, and was instantly cleared by the guards once they saw who was in the vehicle. They opened the gates to the estate and the shuttle continued down the long driveway by road as the pilot switched the sky-to-air vehicle into driving mode.

Serra stared out of the window with nervous anticipation. The Spartan-Rollins' estate was more like a compound than an actual home. The center building was made up of glass and white-stone, set off by a riot of flowers that had been planted surrounding the outside of the main structure. To the right was a large greenhouse, created from glass solar panels and shining steel beams. To the left of the main house were several smaller structures, or what could be considered guest houses, lining the beach-front property.

She remembered being a guest in one of those houses during the years she had been at the training facility. When the recruits had been given leave from the Academy, those who had nowhere to go were welcomed onto the Spartan-Rollins property. Although Serra's family would have allowed her to come home, she had been happier staying close to Jax and Sully whenever it was possible.

They had made a stop at one of the medical centers to deactivate her birth control implant before heading out of the city. She had been nervous about being back in medical, but Jax and Sully had stayed by her side and the procedure only took a matter of minutes to perform. When it was done, they had met Dom and Arik at the shuttle bay and they had gotten into the back while Jax's personal pilot flew them outside the city limits.

A gentle hand took hers, and she looked down to see that Jax had stopped her from tapping her fingers in her nervous habit. "Don't worry, hummingbird. Everything will be fine."

She tried to smile, but knew she failed when his steel-gray eyes softened and he wrapped his arm around her, pulling her closer to his side. "I'm just nervous. I haven't seen your family in a long time."

"They will love you. You know, my mother still invites the recruits to the estate during the breaks from the Academy. Talon is on assignment on Alpha Station: X4, but Connor is still in training. She has her hands full when he and his friends are around."

She laughed. "Sort of like you were. What about Mya? Has she been claimed yet?"

"Hell, no," Archer said with a laugh from her other side. "She just turned twenty, but Jax's fathers got her exempt status when she was seventeen. She doesn't seem like she wants to settle down anytime soon."

"That didn't exactly save me," she said dryly.

Dom laughed from where he was sitting on the other side of the shuttle. The dark man was sprawled out in a chair, eyes remaining closed even as he spoke. "You think any man would be stupid enough to claim the sister of Commander Spartan and the daughter of three powerful parents against her will? They'd be dead before they got the marking device out."

"Damn right," Jax muttered.

"I've heard that Mya is doing well at Starlight Designs," Arik commented. "She seems to have your mother's talent at creating beautiful clothing. Many of the D'Aire wear her designs."

"She is very talented," Jax said, the pride clear in his voice. "She wants to expand the business...sell more to off-worlders. But I hope someday she finds a good bonding unit." He tilted Serra's chin up so he could brush his lips over hers. "I can't wait to have you mark me."

She smiled against his lips. "I like knowing the world will see that you're mine."

"We've always been yours," Archer said as he drew her away from Jax to seal his lips over hers in a heated kiss.

"For the love of...stop it," Dom snapped when he opened his eyes and saw the couple. "If I have to be stuck in here with you, no more of that."

Arik looked at his friend with amusement shining from his iridescent eyes. "Perhaps Serra was right. You do need sex."

"Don't you start with me, you winged bastard," Dom growled. He looked out of the window as the shuttle pulled to a stop in front of the main house right behind another vehicle. "Thank God, we're here."

"Come on, sweetheart," Jax said, grabbing her hand. "Let's go say hello to your new in-laws."

The back door to the shuttle lifted and they walked out to see the occupant of the other vehicle was waiting for them. Troy Takeshi was a handsome man with dark features, short, cropped hair, and a lean body packed with muscle. With a talent for hacking, Troy was a man that Serra trusted and respected, despite the fact he was a few years younger than her. He smiled as he waited for the group to approach at the bottom of the steps.

"Hi, boss," he said to Serra. "I was at my place in Zion, when this primo shuttle pulls up in front of my building, and an officer comes to my door to say my presence is requested for your claiming celebration. Congratulations, Serra, Commander Spartan, Commander Archer."

She smiled affectionately at the other man. "Thank you, Troy. I'm so glad you could come. Actually, I was going to contact you later today about a new project I need your help on."

"Oh?" His dark eyes lit up with interest.

"None of that until tomorrow, after the ceremony is over," Archer chided, then he narrowed his eyes on Takeshi. "But we have something else we want to talk to you about right now."

99

"Murder is not allowed on your claiming celebration day," Dom warned from where he and Arik waited off to the side.

Ignoring him, Jax growled in anger. "What the hell is this I hear about bar hopping and Helios sniffing at our woman?" His furious display lost a little of its edge when Serra's elbow connected with his solar plexus.

"Sir?"

Takeshi was good, Jax had to admit. The younger man didn't give a hint that he knew what he was being asked. "Serra knows we had you assigned to her, but what I want to know is why we never heard about these little excursions she was taking into dangerous places?"

Takeshi's posture stiffened as he went to attention, even as he shot an apologetic glance at Serra. "Sir, as I told you when I was assigned, I would do my duty and keep her safe. But as I also told you, I would not take the position if you were looking for a spy. I work with and respect Serra, and I wouldn't betray her trust like that. Even for you."

Jax admired the younger man's stance, and his respect for the officer grew as he made it clear that he was indeed the perfect assistant for Serra. Still, he didn't want to let the officer off that easily. "You are lucky I don't bust you down to—"

"Enough, Commander. You will not do anything to this officer. Troy is my friend as well as my assistant and I won't take any actions against him lightly. In fact, if you don't drop this right now you may be sleeping alone tonight…and for a long time after this," Serra added.

"Damn, that's cold, baby."

Archer took a step toward Takeshi and held out his hand. The other man hesitated before shaking it. "Thank you for keeping her safe for us."

"She isn't just a duty, she is my friend, too." He turned to look at Serra. "I'm sorry if you feel like I lied to you."

She smiled again. "I knew you were working for them after that first week when you offered to train me in self-defense. I'm not mad."

The front door to the house burst open and Donna Spartan-Rollins hurried down the steps. Her beauty belied her age. It didn't seem possible that the beautiful brunette was the mother of a fully grown man like Jax. Warm brown eyes locked on Serra's a second before she found herself engulfed in a welcoming embrace.

"Serra, how wonderful to see you again!" Donna pressed a kiss to her cheek before she pulled back and held Serra by the shoulders. "Oh, you're more lovely than I remember! My sons are very lucky men."

"It's a pleasure to see you again, Mrs. Spartan-Rollins."

Donna scoffed. "Enough of that, now. You may call me mother just like my boys do, or if it is too soon for that, please just call me Donna." After receiving a nod from Serra, Donna released her to press quick kisses on Jax and Archer's cheek. "Good to see you boys. Now, Serra, come with me. We have to get you ready for the ceremony."

"Ma, I don't think—"

Donna waved off whatever Jax was going to say as Serra found herself being dragged up the stairs by Jax's mother. She sent a frantic look back towards her men.

"Really, can we just—"

At the top of the stairs, Donna turned back to frown down at Archer. "You are going to quit complaining, and go make yourselves useful while I get your chosen ready for the ceremony."

With that, Donna whisked Serra through the doorway and the door slammed shut, leaving the men alone outside. Takeshi looked at his commanders with a hint of pity in his eyes. "Your mother is a formidable woman."

"Kid, you have no idea..." Jax said just as two young officers rounded the corner of the house.

"Commander Spartan!" Officer Cal Ryans, Jax's main assistant, hurried forward. "Sir! The guests you requested have been picked up and are en route. Also, Regent Marks and Regent Wyland-Ross would like a word with you, and so would High Commander Newgate."

"And Commander Archer, there are three generals that would like to speak to you if you have a moment," the other officer added.

Archer blew out a slow breath and looked over at Jax. "I need a drink."

"Make that two."

A little over an hour later, Serra was bathed and dressed in the most gorgeous gown she had ever worn. It was a dress fit for a goddess, made of a shimmering, pale, seafoam green fabric that had one shoulder strap. The garment hugged her body like a second skin, but it was comfortable and allowed her to move easily.

After she had been taken from Jax and Archer's side, Donna had brought Serra up to a suite that had been made ready for the preparations for the ceremony. She had been reunited with Jax's younger sister, Mya, and the young woman had been thrilled that Serra had bonded with Jax and Sully. At Donna's insistence, Serra had been treated to a relaxing massage by a droid expertly programmed in reflexology. Because it was a machine and not another person touching her, Serra was able to settle down and enjoy its ministrations without feeling panicked.

When the massage was over, she was then treated to a luxurious bath with the rare treat of calming crystals from D'Aire. She had been touched when she discovered that the crystals had been a gift from Arik V'Dir. The calming crystals were ridiculously expensive on Earth. They were large salt-like crystals that turned into foam when combined with water, releasing fragrance that soaked into the skin and also had healing properties. The calming crystals could be made with a variety of scents, and in a several different colors. These particular crystals had turned the bath water a pale, frothy purple, and had smelled of citrus and a hint of vanilla.

Serra had used the silk robe left for her and had been surprised when a woman had been waiting with Donna and Mya back in the bedroom. The woman did Serra's make-up with minimal fuss, and then Mya and Donna had presented her with the gown that had been altered for her.

"I ran your measurements through my data unit and made the alterations myself, so I think it should fit you perfectly," Mya had informed her. "I went with this seafoam green because of your eye color and skin tone. I hope you like it."

"Like it? I absolutely love it. Thank you."

A smile shone from eyes the same steel-gray as Jax's as Mya met Serra's gaze in the mirror. "I was right. The dress is perfect on you."

Donna's eyes had a sheen of tears in them as she smiled at Serra. "You are so lovely, Serra. I want to give you this, as your first gift as one of our family."

She opened a large velvet box and Serra let out a gasp as she saw the most beautiful diamond necklace she had ever seen. It was made of small diamonds in a scrolling design set around larger stones in the shape of stars, and a larger star-shaped diamond hung down from the center. Donna removed the necklace from the box and draped it around Serra's neck. The necklace fit snuggly around her throat, and shimmered like pure starlight.

Serra's hand came up to stroke over the stones as she stared at it in awe. "I can't take this. It's too much!"

"Ian's mother gave this to me on the day that I bonded with him and Jack, and someday you will gift it to the woman your first-born son chooses." Donna leaned in and pressed a kiss to Serra's cheek. "I wish you the very best with your bonded…I know you will keep those two in line."

Serra thanked her again, and Donna wiped at a stray tear that she'd lost the battle to hold back. "Enough of that now. I'm going to head downstairs and make sure everything is ready."

Watching as Donna hurried out of the room, Serra couldn't help but wonder how different the moment would be if her own mother had been in attendance. Tania would have found something unkind to say about the way Serra looked or she would have caused some other sort of drama since the event didn't revolve around her. It was safer this way—and to be honest—Serra didn't want her there.

The door to the room clicked open again, and Serra smiled as she saw Skylar Aris slip into the room. Skylar was a beautiful woman, with long, wavy black hair and ice-blue eyes that could unnerve someone just as easily as entice. Serra had met Skylar when they had been in the Academy together. They had become friends since they were both considered outcasts. While Serra was labeled with genius status, Skylar had been tagged with a Class-A Conduit classification. Conduits were the rarest of all the enhanced elites. They were individuals who could basically read other peoples energy, and if they were strong enough, could use that energy for their own purposes by manipulating it.

"Wow, you look absolutely gorgeous!" Skylar beamed at Serra as she hurried forward to give her friend a hug, then she hugged Mya. "Hi, Mya."

"Sky! I'm so happy to see you. I can't believe you're here!"

"Archer contacted me a little while ago. Stars, Serra. I thought if anyone would be safe from being claimed, it would be you. Not that Archer or Jax gave you much say, I'm sure. They've had their eyes on you since we joined the Academy."

Serra laughed. "They did, but I had my eye on them right back."

"I talked to Alexis when I was in transpo on the way over here. She wanted to be here, but they are too far away right now. She said to tell you congrats and that she will see you soon." Skylar pouted for a moment. "Now who is going to be my date for the Freedom Day Gala? Damn it all, who am I going to cause trouble with now that you're shackled with those two hulking beasts?"

Mya perked up at that. "I could attend with you. That way I won't have ten guards trailing after my ass wherever I go. I'd be safe with you."

A slow smile spread over Skylar's face. "Very true. I could just zap whatever idiot was stupid enough to touch you. That's a deal, Mya."

Serra laughed again. "You both could go with real dates."

"Naw, whoever I went with would inevitably annoy me, then I'd have to ditch them or end up shocking them unconscious. But it will be a shame not being able to irritate Jax and Archer after the Gala this year, though." Skylar sighed. "Those were good times."

"What do you mean?"

"Oh, just that every year after we go to the Gala together, I usually get pulled into a meeting with them. They ask me what we did, who we were with, and whatnot."

Serra's eyes went wide. "They did not!"

"Oh, they certainly did. And I usually tell them the same thing…to mind their own damn business. Respectfully, since they are my commanders, but still. It never goes over well, but we both know they had spies watching you anyways."

"Not spies, guards," Mya corrected.

"Same shit," Skylar said, then looked back at Serra. "Holy jump drives, that's some necklace! I guess the guys are pulling out the stops to impress you."

Serra explained how Jax's mother gifted it to her, then had to explain why her own mother wasn't there, careful to leave out any classified data Mya shouldn't know about. It still hurt explaining what Tania had done to her all those years ago, but the pain lessened knowing she was now bonded to the two men who meant the world to her.

"Next time I see Tania, I'm going to zap her dry," Skylar promised darkly.

"She'll be taken care of," Serra replied. She exchanged a look with Skylar that told her friend she would explain more in detail later. Turning back to the mirror, she ran a hand down her dress. "I'm so nervous. I don't know why I'm so nervous when I'm already claimed."

"It's your big day. I've always wanted a sister. I'm so glad they finally claimed you. Speaking of, we should head downstairs now," Mya said when a knock sounded on the door. "Everything should be ready."

The three women left the room and made their way down to the foyer of the main floor to find Jax and Archer waiting for them. Both men were wearing black pants and a button down black shirt with a silver scrolling design on the left side over their muscular chests.

"Aren't you two supposed to be waiting in the room?" Mya asked her brother as she shoved at his arm.

Jax didn't look at his little sister, unable to take his gaze away from the vision that was his chosen. He and Archer had spent the last few hours getting things ready for the ceremony, going along with the plans outlined by his mother, but one thing they would not bend on was coming to collect her personally.

Archer stepped forward, cupping Serra's face in his hands and laid his lips on hers, saying everything he was feeling in the simple gesture. "You are glorious," he said softly when he pulled back. He allowed Jax to steal her from him to wink at Mya before turning to Skylar. "Sky, you may want to avoid Director Stryker and Ambassador V'Dir while you're here. They're a little pissed at you for putting two more of their officers in medical."

Skylar cursed. "It's not my fault their officers are assholes. I have exempt status. I'm not going to feel sorry they got hurt trying to claim me against my will. Stupid men…"

106

She stomped off, muttering to herself as Mya flashed him a grin. "She's like, my hero."

"Stars, save us."

Mya hurried after Skylar, leaving Serra alone with him and Jax. Archer couldn't help but reach out to stroke his hand down Serra's bare arm after Jax stopped kissing her. She looked breathtaking in her dress, with diamonds glittering from around her neck.

"The device you'll use to place the bonding mark on both of us is waiting where the ceremony will be held. It's already been programmed with the tattoo we created, using your initials, along with ours to make up the scroll design," Jax explained. "The tattoo will cover the left side of our torso, neck, shoulder and chest, and it will mark us as yours."

"I like that part."

Archer smiled at her. "I know that we've rushed you into all of this, but you've been ours since we were young. I think it's time you get to show the world that we belong to you."

Serra felt a brief moment of sadness as they walked over to a set of closed double doors, leading to the back of the house. It should have been her fathers walking with her to her claiming ceremony, handing her over to her bonded, but that was not to be. As if knowing something was bothering her, both Jax and Sully squeezed her hands as they paused in front of the closed doors.

"Ready?"

She nodded, then sucked in a breath as they opened the doors.

Chapter Eight

Pure shock had Serra freezing in place.

There before her, waiting on the back terrace were her two fathers, dressed in their formal black uniforms. Cade Lysander and Andrew Dobbs were handsome men, their dark hair marred with a scattering of gray that only made them look more distinguished. She was so caught off guard at the sight of them, she barely noticed the large white tent in the center of the back yard.

"Serra?" Cade Lysander took a tentative step forward, his light-green eyes shining with emotion.

"Dads." Her voice sounded formal, even cold to her own ears, but she couldn't seem to get over the shock enough to react any other way. She watched as both of her fathered flinched, and she clung to Jax and Sully's hands like lifelines as confusion, guilt and pain swamped her. "I'm…shocked to see you here."

"We deserve that," Andrew said, his own brown eyes filled with sorrow. "Oh, baby. We're so very sorry. All this time…"

"When Commander Spartan and Archer contacted us and demanded our presence today, we took the shuttle they sent and arrived, not knowing what to think." Cade's face hardened until it was like stone. "When they told us what your mother did…we *never* knew. I swear it, Serra. All these years, we've begged you to come home and visit, but after we got your last letter, we wanted to respect your wishes. Now, we know it was all a lie to keep you from us. A vicious, hateful lie."

"What letter?" Serra's head was swimming as she tried to understand.

"We received a letter from you two years ago, telling us not to contact you again. That you were happy and there was no place for us in your life anymore. Since you've rarely answered any of our other communications over the years, we thought it was what you wanted."

"I never sent anything like that..." Her throat grew thick with pain. "I did send you a letter two years ago, asking if I could come visit, asking to come home, but your response said you had no place for me and you were too busy. That it wasn't my home anymore."

"We never said that!" Cade whispered harshly. "No matter what has happened over the years, nothing has been more important to us than you."

"You thought I was a freak."

"Never! You were our little girl! Our genius! We were, are, so damn proud of you, but we knew you needed so much more than we could give you. Your mother," Andrew spat out. "That bloody bitch lied and kept you from us. We saved every message, every letter telling us that you were too busy to speak to us or visit. I swear it on my life, Serra. If we knew you wanted us, nothing could have stopped us from coming for you."

A single tear escaped to trail down her pale cheek as she turned to look up at Archer with shattered eyes. "How could she do this to me? To us?"

"I don't know, baby," Archer said softly as he reached out to wipe the tear away. "But they are telling the truth. They both allowed Arik to mind scan them after we told them what your mother had done. In fact, they insisted on it."

"We'll make her pay," Jax vowed.

"Leave Tania to us," Andrew said with deadly conviction. "We have so damn much to pay her back for."

Jax shook his head. "It's not that simple. She broke several Alliance laws by taking Serra to Tartarus, not to mention we need to find out her contact for the drug she used."

"We want in on the investigation."

"Done, but we have to keep your involvement quiet for the time being."

Andrew cleared his throat as he looked back at Serra. "I know we have a lot to talk about and work through, but we would be honored to escort you in to your claiming ceremony right now. It's a day we've dreamed about for a very long time."

"Our baby," Cade said softly as he took another hesitant step forward. "You are so beautiful. I've missed so much watching you grow…"

Serra released Jax and Sully hands to race toward her fathers. Cade met her, sweeping her off her feet as he wrapped his arms around her, burying his face in her neck. Andrew hugged her from behind, so she was surrounded by their love. "Don't cry, baby. You're breaking my heart," Cade whispered, his voice hoarse with his own tears.

"Enough of this for now," Andrew said gruffly as he pulled back and wiped at his own eyes with his sleeves. Turning to Jax and Archer, he nodded to them. "Go inside. We'll bring our girl to you."

Archer nodded, but Jax waited until Serra turned her drenched eyes to him. "Is that alright with you, sweetheart?"

"Yes. My fathers will walk me in." She gave a light laugh. "Just give me a few minutes to fix my make-up."

Jax walked forward until he was standing right in front of her. Tilting her chin up with his fist, he leaned down and brushed his lips over hers. "You are, and always will be, the most beautiful woman in the universe."

He stepped back then shot Cade and Andrew a severe look as Archer kissed her as well. "Guard her well. Even if it is for only a few minutes." With that, Jax turned and walked down the few steps heading toward the white tent with Archer.

"Your bonded are very intense men," Andrew said.

"They are," she agreed with a little chuckle.

Cade and Andrew shared a look over her head, then smiled down at her. "We will never really let you go, Serra. Never. We've loved you all your life, and we will continue to love you until the day we die. You'll always be our little girl."

A mischievous gleam sparkled in Andrews eyes. "And we aren't losing a daughter. They are gaining two more fathers to deal with."

She was still laughing when the escorted her down to the front of the white tent. The sky was a brilliant cascade of colors as the sun began sinking into the horizon, turning the water into sparkling red and gold glass. She took a moment to remember spending time down on the beach when she visited during her breaks from the Academy.

The memory made her smile.

"Are you ready, Serra?" Cade asked.

"I am." Taking a deep breath, she tried to calm the riot of emotions swirling around inside of her belly before they lifted the opening and walked inside.

The interior of the tent was dark, but the glow of a thousand candles filled the space with a soft, amber light, giving it an almost magical feel. There were dozens of people inside, all sitting in chairs fashioned into a large circle around a raised platform in the center. She knew they had tried to keep the celebration small—so Serra's mother wouldn't hear about the claiming—but that didn't seem to stop Jax's mother from putting together a top-tier list of guests.

Among the crowd, she could see several formal red uniforms worn by the members of the Council of Regents, along with the white uniforms of two high commanders. Serra also saw her friends Troy and Skylar, as well as Officers Meyers and Rhine, her two guards that had been cleared of suspicion.

Serra held onto her fathers' arms as they guided her forward to the center of the room, where Jax and Sully were waiting for her. Her gaze locked with theirs, and she felt her nerves disappear as her love for them washed through her. She went to them, with the scent of spring kissing her skin and warmth in her heart. When she was standing in front of them, she placed her hands in theirs, smiling up into their serious faces. She barely heard Regent Ian Spartan and

Jack Rollins as they spoke to the crowd, welcoming everyone and thanking them for coming to celebrate with them. Donna stepped forward and handed the marking device to Serra.

"Welcome to our family," Donna whispered as she squeezed Serra's hand, then the older woman took Ian and Jack's hands and they left the platform.

Serra looked down at the device in her hand then back up at her men as they stripped off their shirts, displaying their bare muscular chests. The moment felt so solemn, so enormous with what it meant for them. Don't screw this up, she told herself.

"Serra Spartan-Archer, we have claimed you as our chosen," Jax said in a loud, clear voice. "We pledge ourselves to you, and ask to wear your mark to show the world we are a bonded unit. Serra, I loved you as a boy, and now I love you as a man. As you wear my mark, I will wear yours. There will never be another for me. I promise to honor, love and care for you, until I take my very last breath."

Tears stung her eyes at his words. Jax was such a tough, commanding man, but had spoken from his heart, not hesitating to tell the entire room what she meant to him. He was her warrior, and he was her shield. Jax would always stand in front of her if she were in danger, but he would stand by her side and be her partner, too. There was passion and fire between them, but there was also love. She took a step toward him, and he held his arms slightly away from his body to allow her to run the device along his neck and torso. He's mine, she thought after the mercurial black design covered the left side of his body.

Serra gasped as Jax gripped her by the back of the neck and hauled her close enough for his mouth to capture hers. His kiss was deep, hot and possessive, instantly setting her body on fire as lust slammed into her.

"For the love of…"

She heard one of her father's muttering and a smatter of laughter from the crowd, reminding her they were not alone. She pushed at Jax's chest until he released her, and tried to hold back a smile. "Behave," she whispered.

"Not bloody likely."

A little snicker escaped before she got control of herself again. Turning to Sully, she saw he was waiting for her with love shining in his light-brown eyes. Moving closer, she trailed a hand lightly over his bare chest and watched his muscles flex at her touch.

"You are my soul mate, my other half. Serra, you are mine, as I've always been yours, and I'll wear your mark with pride. I promise to honor, love and care for you...until forever and a day."

He was right. Sully was her soul mate. He was her comfort, and he was her protector. He would always put her first, and give her what she needed. They had affection and tenderness between them that burned hot from the intensity of devotion they felt for one another. She held up the device and ran it along his neck and torso, marking him as her bonded. When the tattoo was complete, she stepped into his kiss, parting her lips to stroke her tongue against his.

With the blood in her veins singing with excitement, she stepped back in order to look at both of her men. Seeing their combined initials worn on their skin filled her with joy. She thought it was a powerful statement...and she also found the marks surprisingly arousing.

They were hers...every delicious inch of them.

A thought flickered through her mind, and going with impulse, she held up her hand before Jax could speak again. "I know this isn't normally done, but I'd also like to wear our mark on my arm so we match," she said, lowering her voice so only they would hear.

Surprised had both men's eyes widening. "Are you sure, Serra?"

"I am. I don't want it on my neck, just my arm. Would that be all right?"

Jax's eyes narrowed as his gaze skimmed over her bare left arm, as if trying to imagine the mark on her skin. "Archer, can you

114

switch the initials so ours are bigger on her, and decrease the lines so they're more delicate?"

"Sure can," Archer said, taking the marking device from her.

"Does it hurt?" she asked softly. She didn't remember since she hadn't been conscious the first time they used the device to claim her.

Jax reached up and stroked a fingertip lightly against their mark near her eye as if he were remembering it as well. "You'll feel a little tingle, but it shouldn't hurt you. You really want to do this for us? You already wear our mark on your face."

"I do. I like knowing that when people see it they will know we are truly a unit with matching marks." Then going with complete honesty, she added, "But I also find the marks on you quite arousing, and figured you might have the same reaction seeing it on me."

"Hell fucking yes we will," Jax growled.

"Done," Archer said after he'd recalibrated the device. Ignoring the murmurs in the crowd, he focused hot eyes on Serra. "Just thinking about seeing this on you is making me hard."

"You always seem to be hard," she whispered back, smiling.

"Only when I'm around you," he said with a wink, then he handed the device to Jax.

It was like this had somehow been meant to be. The dress she wore left her arm and shoulder completely bare on left side. Serra took both of Sully's hands in hers, gripping them tight as Jax moved to her side holding the device.

"Are you ready, sweetheart?"

"First, let me say something. I've loved both of you before I even knew what love truly was. You have been my constants, my tethers to a world I don't really understand. With you, I don't feel lost anymore. I'm glad that you claimed me, and I'm proud to be your chosen. Okay, I'm ready now."

Jax stared at her intensely for a moment before he held the marking device up to her skin and they heard the crowd gasp in surprise. Serra felt her arm tingle with the pressure of the marking. It didn't hurt, but it did feel strange. Sully squeezed her hands harder, as if to stop her from pulling away. She smiled up at him. "I'm fine."

"You're better than fine. You're perfect."

"And you belong to us," Jax whispered as he finished the tattoo.

She looked down to see the tattoo design was similar to theirs, but it wasn't exactly the same. The scrolling lines were not as thick as they were on their arms, and instead of her large initials in the center of the mark, Sully had somehow created a new design that almost looked as if their initials were surrounding and protecting hers. The symbolism wasn't lost on her.

The tattoo was beautiful, and she loved it.

Archer put down the marking device and took one of Serra's hands, while Jax took hold of the other. As a unit, the three of them stood, sharing the moment.

"It's done," Archer said, his voice rough with emotion.

"No," Serra whispered back. "It's only just beginning."

Two hours later, Jax was out of patience.

After the ceremony, the guests had been escorted back into the main house where an elaborate dinner was to be held. It had brought him a sort of primal satisfaction to see their claim on her, and it had been a struggle not to pick her up and carry her away so the three of them could be alone. He'd wanted to say fuck the dinner, but the way Serra's face lit up when she had learned what his mother had planned for them had made him bite back his impatience.

He and Archer had put their shirts back on, resigned to the fact they would have to wait to get Serra alone. Forced to be social, Jax had been pleased to watch Serra enjoy herself throughout the meal, and talking to the guests after they were done eating. He knew she was usually uneasy around strangers and in large crowds, but she seemed to do well enough as long as he or Archer remained by her side.

They had introduced Serra to many of the guests she didn't know, but there were some that she had met before her mother had taken her away from them. Jax's youngest brother, Connor, had been thrilled to see her again, and it warmed his heart by the way she seemed at ease with his family. He had also introduced her to Connor's best friend, Simon. It made Jax proud that Connor had befriended the young man he and Archer had helped gain entry into the Academy only months ago.

Simon and his little sister had been found in the badlands by their friend Alexis and her four Dragon Warrior mates. When they discovered the two teens were being abused by their father, Alexis had sent the teens to Jax and Archer, who had made sure they found a new home within the Alliance. Like it had been with Jax and Archer when they were young, Connor had instantly formed a friendship with Simon, and the two were practically inseparable now. When they came of age, Jax had no doubt that Connor and Simon would make a powerful elite pair.

Marissa, Simon's sister, was also a guest, and Jax knew his mother had taken an interest in ensuring the youngster had found happiness after suffering such an awful childhood. The young girl seemed to blossom now that she had gotten over her initial fear of the Alliance. It made Jax angry that so many people in the badlands misunderstood the Alliance and what they stood for. He blamed the rebels for that. They spread their lies and caused problems out in the areas the Alliance didn't monitor closely.

But that wasn't something Jax wanted to think about tonight.

Now, Jax was sitting back in his chair as both of his fathers' voices drolled on about something or other. He tuned them out, watching Archer dance with their chosen, loving the way her body moved in that dress that looked like it had been painted on her. She was so fucking beautiful that she stole his breath each time he looked at her. He wanted her, God, how he wanted her.

And now she truly belonged to them.

Jax wasn't a man who allowed himself to get over emotional, but she had almost brought him to his knees when she'd asked to have the bonding marks put on her arm so she matched them. It had stunned him and filled him with pride that she wanted the world to have no doubt about who she belonged to, and his hands had shook a little before he had regained enough control to put the mark on her.

Serra was a fascinating woman. At times she was so vulnerable. With her little quirks she saw as flaws, he only saw them as things that made her more special. She was brilliant, ranking higher than even most geniuses, but he didn't mind she was smarter than they were. Hell, the truth was, he was just a soldier at heart, and it amazed him that she could be happy with a couple of elites when she could do so much better. Not that either he or Archer would ever give her up. His chest tightened as he thought about all of the years that had been stolen from them, and he vowed that her mother would pay for every single second they had lost.

Now, he was done waiting.

If he didn't get his dick inside of his woman soon, he thought he might fucking die.

"Jax, are you listening to me?"

"No," Jax said curtly, standing up. "I love you both, but I'm leaving."

Regent Ian Spartan and Jack Rollins grinned at each other. "I told you he wouldn't last another hour."

"I take it back. I hate you both," Jax growled out, then stalked away from the table as both of his fathers started laughing. When Officer Ryans hurried up to him, he simply snarled, and had the poor man running for cover. Jax reached Serra and Archer, and he pressed up against her back, caging her between them. "We have to go. Now."

118

"I was wondering when you would break," Archer said, his eyes alight with amusement.

"I fucking mean it. Right now."

With a laugh, Serra turned to him and wound her arms around his neck. He lost himself looking down into her light-green eyes, and let out a groan as he took her mouth in a kiss that both teased and tormented him.

"Yeah, it's time to go," Archer said softly.

As a unit, the three of them quickly made their way outside, barely stopping to say goodbye to anyone before heading to a hover-cart that was parked in front of the house. Jax got behind the wheel and turned it on as Archer snuggled Serra onto his lap in the passenger seat. When the cart lifted into the air, Jax flew them down the path towards the last guest house on the estate, pushing the small vehicle to its limits.

"Come on, hummingbird," Archer said as he lifted her in his arms after the hover-cart came to a stop. He waited for Jax to open the door, then carried her into the dark house.

"Wait right here," Jax commanded as he turned on the lights, then bounded up the stairs, out of view.

"He's so bossy."

Smiling at her playful tone, Archer leaned down to press a soft kiss to her lips. Carrying her over to one of the sofas, he sat down with her in his lap. "You knew making him wait to have you after you marked us would drive him crazy, but you love that, don't you?"

"What? Driving you both crazy?"

"Yeah."

"Maybe," she said fluttering her lashes. "But we couldn't just leave our own party. Not after all the work Donna did to make today so special."

"It was special, but now we're going to have our own little celebration," Archer murmured as he brushed his lips over hers again. "Are you ready to take us both, Serra? Will you let us both pleasure you tonight?"

Worry flashed in her pretty green eyes, then he saw the determination set in. "I am. Sully...I know the fundamentals of what it will entail, but I can't help but be concerned about the actual process."

He let out a laugh. "God, woman! You undo me. Don't worry about the process. We'll help you through it, and at any time if you're uncomfortable or want to stop, all you have to do is tell us. You know we would never hurt you. Do you remember when we were here that first summer you were at the Academy with us? That first day on the beach?"

Serra's fingers played with the collar of his shirt. "I remember. I was so scared of everything, and the other students were so mean to me when you, Jax, Sky or Alexis weren't around. I was crying down on the beach when you found me that day." She looked up into his eyes, and there was wonder in them now. "You came and sat with me, and told me you would always be there for me if I needed you. And you have been. Even when you weren't physically there, you were with me."

Archer felt he heart swell in his chest at the absolute trust he saw shining back at him. "There you were, such a sad little girl with such old eyes. Eyes that showed the intelligence burning inside of you. People just didn't understand you then, but I did. It was like my soul recognized yours. I knew you were special, but at the time I didn't know exactly how special. But that day on the beach, I knew I never wanted to see tears in your eyes again."

"I fell in love with you that day. You were my hero," she said with a smile. "I was too young to understand what I was feeling, but I knew how I felt when I was with you and Jax."

"How did you feel?"

"Safe. Safe and cared for. I'd never felt that way before. Not really."

"We will always keep you safe," he swore. His hand fisted in her hair, dragging her closer so he could plunder her mouth. God, the taste of her. He was like a man dying of hunger, and only she could sate his need. Serra was so fucking precious to him. The way she'd given herself to them today by taking their combined mark on her arm had filled a part of his soul that had been empty before her. The need to belong. To truly belong and be accepted for who he was.

Jax and his family had taken Archer in when he was young, but there had always been a little part of him that remained on the outside. It was from knowing that he would never come first in someone's life. But with Serra, he finally had that. What she gave him was equal to what she gave Jax. Although it was slightly different for each, she held nothing back with either of them, and her love completed them both.

She was the missing piece they had both been looking for.

Chapter Nine

"Okay! Come on up!"

Archer stood up, still cradling Serra in his arms and made his way slowly up the stairs. "We are going to love on you so hard tonight, you'll pass out from the pleasure."

"I hope not. I'd like to remain conscious for the fun."

He was chuckling as they entered the bedroom Jax had prepared for their use. He turned to watch the shocked delight cross over Serra's face, and gave Jax a silent nod of approval. Since they had seen the way her eyes had all but danced with appreciation when she'd seen the tent lit up with candlelight earlier, Jax had placed candles on every flat surface of the bedroom, creating a romantic ambiance, complete with silky rose petals of red, white and pink he had scattered over the bed.

"Oh, Jax…"

Archer lowered her feet to the ground, so she could go to Jax. It always struck him as odd that he didn't feel the slightest pang of jealously watching his woman go to her other lover. Perhaps it was because he and Jax were so close they were almost like an extension of each other, but he thought the real reason was that having two lovers ensured she would always be protected.

Serra's hands brushed up the broad expanse of Jax's bare chest until she clasped them around his neck, drawing his head down to hers. She kissed him sweetly, thanking him for the care he had put into making the setting perfect for their first night together as a bonded unit. He had taken off his shirt and shoes, but had left his pants on. Feeling the hard, thick column of his rigid cock against her stomach, she pressed closer, and was rewarded as he took their kiss deeper.

She answered his urgency with her own, wanting more…needing more. Hard hands gripped her arms, pushing her back against Sully's bare chest. "Slow it down, sweetheart."

Both men stroked their hands over her arms and shoulders, soothing her while their light touch stroked the fires of her lust for them with a kind of ruthless tenderness.

"You did all this for me." Her statement was filled with wonder. No one had ever made her feel as special as Jax and Sully did, and she knew no one ever would.

"Don't you know yet there is nothing we wouldn't do for you?"

"Thank you."

"You have to learn to stop thanking us. Your love is all we need."

"I do love you, Jax," she whispered.

She saw the hunger burning in his steel-gray eyes, turning them molten with a mixture of love and passion. He raised a hand, rubbing his thumb over her lower lip, caressing it slowly. "I knew you were meant to be ours. No amount of distance or time could ever change that."

Sully trailed a hand down the mark on her arm. "She belongs to us now, Jax."

"She does," Jax said, his voice filled with satisfaction.

"You belong to me, too," she reminded them. "Both of you do."

"We do, and now we are going to prove it. This is what is going to happen. First, we are going to strip you naked, so I can eat that sweet, little pussy until you come."

"Then it's my turn," Archer said before nipping lightly at her neck with his teeth. It didn't hurt, but was just enough to make her shiver. "I'm going to make you come again so you're nice and soft, and so very wet for us. Once you are, we're going to take you…together."

"You both talk too much," she panted out, making them both chuckle. She wanted them to shut the hell up and get on with it, but she also enjoyed letting the anticipation build, heightening her arousal.

"Do we? You like when we talk dirty to you, don't you, Serra? I bet hearing what we want to do to you has made you wet. Shall we see if I'm right?"

Jax pushed the single shoulder strap of the dress down her arm as Archer helped tug the material lower until the shimmering fabric fell in a pool at her feet. Both men inhaled sharply, and Jax's eyes smoldered like a waiting storm. "Are you fucking kidding me? You were naked under that damn dress the entire night?"

Jutting her chin out, she met his gaze. That dark gleam in his eyes made her clench her thighs together to stop the liquid heat from spilling from her pussy. Stars, she loved it when he got all possessive. Nothing made her hotter. "Are you really going to complain now?"

"If I'd known, you would have found yourself fucked before we sat down to dinner."

That made her laugh. "Which is why I didn't tell you."

Sully's deep voice lowered to a seductive rumble as one of his hands reached around her to splay over her belly. "No complaints here, baby. Why don't you kick off those shoes…that's our girl."

His other hand cupped her breast as he held her against him, pinching the nipple lightly so it puckered into a hard nub. She could feel the steel-spike of his erection poking into her back, and it made her shiver with awareness. She was mesmerized by the intensity in Jax's gray eyes as he watched her. He seemed to be fighting something inside himself, and she found herself wishing he would just let go. She sensed the raw power coiled in his body, and knew when he unleashed it she'd be in for a wild ride.

"Tell us what you want, Serra."

"I want you. Both of you."

"And you'll have us. But I want to hear what you want. In graphic detail. Say it, and we'll give it to you."

Frustration battled with arousal as she huffed out a breath. "I want your hands and your mouths on me. I want you to make me come."

"Good girl. Spread your legs," Jax growled out. "Wider."

She did as he asked and widened her stance, showing him the gleaming flesh of her core. She knew her pussy was slick with her juices, proving he had been right, that their words already had her on edge.

"She's already soaking wet, Archer."

Serra found herself melting back into Sully, leaning against his strong, muscular body as Jax stroked two of his fingers over the slick folds of her pussy. She felt her legs tremble as he pushed those thick digits into her, filling her, sliding through the proof of her desire for them. Her body clenched around him, grasping greedily, wanting more as her body arched into his touch.

"That's it, sweetheart. Let me in. Let me give you what you need."

Unable to look away from him, her eyes went wide as he went to his knees in front of her. Color flooded her cheeks as she looked down at him. Her protest died on a moan as he dove straight in to suck on her clit as he began to thrust his fingers in and out of her tight hole. He shoved her thighs further apart as they tried to close. She could feel the pressure building inside her, fast and hard. She tried to move, but was held in place by Sully. She tried to brace herself against the onslaught of pleasure, but neither man gave her the option of holding back.

Sully turned her head, claiming her lips in hot kiss. Forcing them apart, his tongue plunged deep, stroking and tasting. Her mind went blank. It was impossible to think as Sully's hands cupped her full breasts, drinking in her cries as Jax ruthlessly pushed her into a quick, vicious climax.

Brutal ecstasy hit her like a turbo-jet, sending shockwaves of pleasure pulsing through her system. Her knees buckled, but Sully quickly caught her in his arms before she fell, and carried her over to the bed. He laid her down, then pulled her body to the edge of the bed, sinking down in front of her so his face was between her legs.

126

"Fuck, you are so beautiful when you come, baby." He smiled, a wicked gleam in his eyes. "Now it's my turn."

Her lashes fluttered open, but her mouth was claimed in a searing kiss by Jax before she could say a word. His lips fused to hers, giving and taking pleasure in equal measure until she was practically mad with need. She tasted herself on him, and it only added to the intimacy between them. Her body jerked as Sully's tongue thrust into her tight pussy, lapping up the juices spilling from her. He pushed her thighs further apart, making room for his broad shoulders.

Sharp, sexual need had her hips bucking. She tried to fight back the pleasure Sully was forcing on her, but there was no use. Like Jax, Sully knew exactly how to play her body. He alternated licking and sucking, making her crazy as he teased her.

Jax pulled back, looking down at her. He could hardly believe that she was really there with them. She was theirs. Theirs to take, to pleasure…to love. And she always would be. Emotions surged through him, filling his entire body with the love he felt for her. His cock strained against the confines of his pants, wanting to be free. Wanting to be inside of Serra. He and Archer had agreed to keep their pants on until they were ready to take her, neither of them wanting to overwhelm her.

But Serra seemed to be handling them just fine.

She was so beautiful with her dark-brown hair was fanned out around her like some sort of dark halo amidst the sea of rose petals. Those big, light-green eyes stared up at him, glazed with passion, and he knew it was a picture he would always keep with him.

She looked…utterly magnificent.

Jax gazed down at the perfection of her soft skin splayed out before him, and his mouth watered at the sight of her hard nipples. He allowed himself a taste, and moaned as he sucked one into his mouth, then the other. He drew back, circling a finger around the wet nub of one nipple, watching it harden even more. "Does that feel good, sweetheart? Is Archer making you feel good?"

"God, yes!"

"He's going to make you come again. You're going to—" His words cut off on a growl as she reached out and gripped his cock hard through the fabric of his pants.

"You talk too much," she ground out.

Amusement warred with lust as she stroked him, holding onto his cock as Archer drove her own body higher. "You want my cock, Serra?"

"Yes. Take your pants off. Sully, if you don't stop teasing me I may have to hurt you. I need to come!"

Serra gasped as Sully began licking and sucking her with more force, giving her exactly what she'd asked for. She began chanting his name, felt the tremors begin, then her body simply shattered as she came.

Jax slid off the bed to remove his pants as he watched their woman writhing in ecstasy on the bed. He freed himself, allowing his cock to spring out, hard and thick. When he was completely naked, he stood still, allowing Serra to look her fill. He knew she loved looking at their bodies, how fascinated she was by their differences. The hunger in her eyes made him feel like a god, and he felt a pulse of pre-cum leaking from the head of his cock as her gaze stroked over him like a phantom caress.

He took his shaft in his hand, stroking himself, spreading the drops of pre-cum over the head. "You want my cock, Serra? Is this what you want…what you're aching for?"

"Yes, Jax…"

Serra watched Jax smirk at her, then she gasped as Sully gripped her hips and thrust his own cock inside her without warning.

"See what happens when you don't pay attention?" Archer scolded.

Smirking, he lowered his large body onto her, pressing against her as he sought her mouth with his. She wound her arms around his back, holding him to her. Serra loved the feel of his hard body pressing down on her, loved feeling the muscles of his back straining beneath her hands as he began moving inside of her. She opened for him, welcomed him in.

She took the pleasure he gave her, and gave back more.

Archer felt the rush of desire, that sharp slap of acute satisfaction as she surrounded him. As she took him into her. He fought back the need to come, wanting to prolong the pleasure. Her pussy was like a tight vise around his cock, firmly gripping him as he pushed through tense muscles so he was fully sheathed inside her wet heat. He felt her legs and arms holding onto him as if she never wanted to let go, as if he would leave her now that he was exactly where he wanted to be.

He stared into her gorgeous eyes, watched the passion blazing back at him so strong he felt burned alive by the green flames. His mouth took hers again, capturing her gasp as he flexed his hips, sliding back, then shoving deep into her pussy, filling her with all of him again.

Sensing his friend's impatience, Archer held onto Serra as he rolled them over on the bed so she was straddling him. Her eyes grew wide, and he could see the apprehension creep in. "No, baby. Don't tense up on us now. Will you let us love you together? Are you ready to share this with us?"

"I…I think so. Can you just…can we just take it slow?"

Jax stroked his hands over the smooth, silky skin of her back, wanting to calm her. "I'll go slow. Don't worry, sweetheart. We'll take care of you. I just have to get you ready first, then we can love you together."

He picked up the small tube of lubrication he had placed on the bed, and poured some into his hand, making sure his fingers were completely coated. He made a soothing sound as he felt her jerk when he stroked a slick finger over her back hole, pushing in a little to work the tight entrance open.

Archer gripped her face, making her focus on him as Jax continued to prepare her to take them both. "Hard and fast, or soft and slow. Anyway we take you, it's us loving you."

"I know...I'm just...it feels weird."

Jax pressed two fingers inside her, working her open for him. She was so damn tight, and her muscles fought him as he stretched her with his fingers. "This is new for you. Just relax and let me get you ready. You're going to feel different having me here, but it's going to be even more intense with Archer filling your tight, little pussy while I push inside you. It will feel better than anything you've ever experienced before."

"So you say..." she muttered as she wiggled into a more comfortable position, making Archer groan as his cock jerked inside her.

"Jax, she's too tight. I'm not going to last long."

Jax pulled his fingers out of her, then used a liberal amount of the lube to coat his cock. She flinched as he poured more of the slippery liquid directly onto her ass, working it inside of her as he felt Archer's cock pulse and throb through the thin membrane that separated her two channels.

Serra trembled as Jax got in position behind her. She felt the large head of his cock settle against the tight rosebud of her ass, and couldn't stop her body from shaking as adrenaline and fear rushed through her.

"Just relax, baby. Here we go..."

Jax began to press against the small hole, pushing his cock against her gently to gain entrance. Serra's body clenched reflexively, trying to keep him from entering her, but he wouldn't be deterred. He waited for her to relax again, then pushed harder, feeling her muscles give way, letting the head of his cock pop into her tight, hot hole. The slick liquid allowed his entire cock to slide deep, and his own groan mixed with her sharp gasp of pain. Once he was all the way inside her, he froze.

"Doing okay, Serra?"

"That hurt, but it's fading now. Just…wait a minute."

"Anything you need."

Jax knew—like with any new experience—he had to give her time to acclimate to the new sensations bombarding her. He had to allow her to assimilate what she was feeling before he pushed her too far…even if it fucking killed him. And it quite possibly would. Her ass was so tight, it bordered on pain as she clamped around him. Sweat poured down Jax's face as he waited. He tried to focus on Archer as he whispered to Serra, but nothing could distract Jax from the exquisite torture of having his cock all the way inside her tight ass.

"Oh, wow…"

"How do you feel, baby?" Archer asked as he pressed kisses over her face.

"So full. I feel so full with both of you inside me. It hurt at first. Burned, but now there is just a dull ache. I honestly don't know if I like it or not…yet."

Jax needed to move, to pull out so he could surge back inside her, but he couldn't, wouldn't do that before she was ready. Desperately needing to distract her, Jax reached around and began rubbing his slick fingers over her clit, hoping to switch her discomfort back into pleasure.

"Like that do you?" Jax asked with a chuckle when she moaned.

"That definitely helps."

Taking that as a good sign, Jax continued to stroke her clit with his fingers as he pulled out a little, then pushed back in.

"Oh!"

"Was that a good or bad oh?"

"Good…I think."

"Then just relax and let us pleasure you," Archer whispered, kissing her deep. Lifting his hips, he pushed his cock more firmly inside her pussy, then pulled back out as Jax began to slowly move in counter-point. She was so tight, felt so good he thought he would go absolutely mad with the pleasure.

Lowering his body over her, Jax pressed hot, wet kisses over her shoulders. "You feel so good, Serra. Your ass is tighter, smoother, and so damn hot you feel like you're going to singe my cock right off."

"But your pussy is just as tight. It's squeezing me so hard I could come right now just feeling you pulse around me," Archer added as he rotated his hips on his next thrust. He studied her carefully as they moved inside her. "You okay, baby?"

"It's so good," she whispered. "Love you. Love you both. Now show me. Show me all the pleasure you can give me."

With a groan, Archer pulled her head down so he could plunge his tongue back into her mouth, stroking and tasting. He wrapped his arms around her tight, anchoring her to him as he met Jax's eyes over her shoulder.

With a nod, Jax took control. Gripping her hips, he pulled back, then thrust forward, filling her again. He repeated the motion over and over again, thrusting into her with a steady rhythm that had all three of them gasping.

"Sully! Jax!" Serra let out a low moan as her body went into lockdown. The orgasm tore through her like a meteor, making her clamp down around their thrusting shafts. She couldn't stop the tears from leaking from her eyes, and wouldn't even if she could. Overwhelmed with emotions, lost in the pleasure, she gave herself over to them, trusting them to keep her safe.

"Fucking hell, did you feel that," Archer gasped out.

"She's like a fucking vise," Jax curse as he sped up the pace, pounding himself into her ass so the bed shook with the force of each thrust. Feeling her clench around him shattered the rest of his control. A primal urgency surged through his bloodstream, driving him on. He gripped her hips hard, holding her still for his thrusts, hard enough to bruise flesh, but he couldn't seem to stop himself.

"Jax, I can't hold back any longer," Archer groaned out.

"I'm close, too. Come again, Serra. Come and take us with you."

"I don't think I can!"

"Yes, you can. Don't fucking hold back on us. Give in," he snarled. Reaching down between her and Archer again, he used two fingers to ruthlessly work her clit as he continued to pound his cock into her. "Come for us, Serra. Come now!"

Serra felt the world fracture as she came apart again. Held safe between them, she cried out and let herself fly.

Archer groaned out her name as he exploded inside her, filling her pussy with pulse after pulse of his hot seed. His arms wrapped around her tight, so tight he feared he was squeezing the breath right out of her, but he needed to feel her pressed against him as his body jerked.

Jax pumped inside her once, twice more, then shudders racked his body as he buried his face in her neck, pouring himself into her as the most intense pleasure he'd ever known shook him to his very soul. He caught himself before he fell on her, his legs weak with lethargy from his brutal climax. He took a long moment to catch his breath, pressing one last kiss to her shoulder before he pulled out of her and walked to the bathroom to clean up.

Serra collapsed on Sully, barely stirring as he stroked the wet strands of hair from her face. Content to simply lay there, her eyes remained closed as she listened to the rapid thud of his heart. She smiled, letting herself bask in the afterglow of their spectacular lovemaking.

Her satisfied little bubble was disturbed when she felt a warm, wet cloth between her legs. Opening one eye, she lifted her head just enough to blink down at Jax in question.

"What's that look for, sweetheart? I'm not doing anything nefarious back here. I'm just cleaning you."

"After what we just did, I have a right to be suspicious, don't I?"

Both Jax and Sully snickered, and Serra pinched Sully in retribution at having her perch disturbed when she almost fell off him. He winced, then kissed her forehead. "Sorry, baby."

When she was clean, Jax went back into the bathroom as Serra snuggled back into Sully's arms. "I have to admit, it's times like this I'm damn glad we have these enhancements. I barely feel any discomfort at all. I enjoyed it, after that first moment of 'what the fuck' was over."

Jax laughed as he rejoined them on the bed. "It will get better the more you get used to it."

"That is so like a man to say something stupid like that."

"What? It's true."

She turned her head to eye him with speculation. "Are you saying this from experience?"

Jax's eyes narrowed. "No."

She smiled. "Then your statement is being disregarded for lack of empirical substantiation."

"You know how hard it gets me when you use big words," Archer growled playfully as he nipped at her lips.

"Come on, little genius," Jax said as he lifted her into his arms. "You may be feeling okay, but I bet you'll feel even better after a nice, hot bath."

She rested her head on his shoulder. "You're pampering me."

"We're full service."

"Will you stay with me?"

"Sweetheart, you couldn't keep us away," he said, then pressed his lips firmly to hers.

Chapter Ten

Archer studied the screen of his data unit through narrowed eyes that were heavy with fatigue. It had been four days since they had left the Spartan-Rollins estate and traveled back to their residence in the heart of the Capital. After their amazing claiming ceremony, it had been time to get back to work on figuring out who the hell was behind the potential sale of the stealth tech, so they could shut them down.

Their quarters had become a base of operations, which irritated him even though he knew it was necessary. People seemed to constantly come and go, filling the normally quiet space with noise and voices as they held strategy meetings and talked over the details. Jax, Jack Rollins, Cade Lysander and Dominic Stryker were working together in Jax's office, while Archer ran his own data in his office next door with High Commander Roman Newgate and Andrew Dobbs.

They left the connecting door between the rooms open, and he could hear Regent Spartan and Arik V'Dir talking in the central living room where they had created a makeshift workspace. Officer Ryans played runner between the three areas, making sure everyone had what they needed. It wasn't exactly the way Archer had planned spending the first week as a bonded unit with Serra, and that added to his irritation. He'd had very little time alone with her since they'd been back, but he seemed to be handling it a little better than Jax.

Thinking about his friend, Archer absently wondered how long it would take his partner to snap. Who could really blame either of them for being annoyed when both of Jax's fathers, as well as Serra's, had all but moved into their damn residence? Arik and Dom were there just as often, and even High Commander Newgate seemed to show up for hours at a time. They couldn't exactly boot any of the men out, but he wished like hell that they could.

They'd all missed the activities that had been held throughout the Capital for the week long Freedom Day's celebration. Each year, the entire world honored the day that Earth defeated the Zyphir and ended the Alien Wars, with the help of their allies, of course. Archer and Jax usually skipped most of it anyways, and Serra hated the crowds, but it would have been nice to enjoy some of those events together and just…be. There would always be next year, he reminded himself, and all the years that followed since they now had a lifetime together.

Looking out of the main door of his office, he glanced into the room across the hall where they had created an office/lab for Serra. From his chair he studied her as she focused on her data unit next to Troy Takeshi. Archer had given up trying to understand what she was doing within a few hours after they had been working on their first day back. She had been right about the code she used. It was like trying to read some archaic cipher. He had to give credit to Takeshi for learning how to understand what looked to him to be a garble of numbers and letter that made absolutely no sense whatsoever.

Serra had put her hair up in one of those intricate winding deals, held together with some sort of clip so it wouldn't get in her way. Her light-green eyes burned with some inner fire, obviously energized by whatever she was working on. She didn't seem to mind the chaos or the noise. It fascinated Archer by the way she was able to block out everything but the project she was working on. She'd been the same way when they were growing up, but now that focus had intensified, making everything else around her obsolete.

But where Archer understood, and was even amused by her focus, Jax wasn't taking her dismissal well at all.

Noticing the time, Archer pushed up from his desk, and headed out to the dining room. He saw Regent Spartan and Arik both on their wrist units, talking to their contacts in clipped tones. Ignoring them, he moved over to the food console to program some provisions for the troops. Taking a moment to be eternally grateful to Officer Ryans, who coordinated all of the other assistants both Archer and Jax had working for them, he noticed that the food console was stocked full with a variety of food and drinks, in amounts that were enough to feed an army…which they basically were at this point.

Archer pulled out large plates filled with food and began setting them onto the buffet table located against the wall. At the scent of food the men drifted out of the offices, sniffing at the air. "Ah, damn good idea," Andrew Dobbs said as he walked up.

"You know, you all have your own food back at your own homes," Jax growled as he frowned at them.

"We do, but it's so much more satisfying eating yours," Dom said with a smile as he bit down into a sandwich. "Damn, this is real roast beef."

"You're a freaking director. You have enough credits to buy your own roast beef."

"I do, but why should I when I can just eat yours?"

"Bastard."

Archer chuckled as they continued their banter, turning to Officer Cal Ryans as the other man started helping transferring the food to the buffet table. "Officer Ryans?"

"Yes, sir?"

"Thank you."

The young man's eyebrows winged up. "Sir?"

Stars, were they really such assholes that the damn kid was shocked speechless that Archer thanked him? Holding back a grimace, he realized they were. It was Serra's fault, always thanking everyone for every damn thing. She was a bad influence…or good. He sighed. "You always take care of things before we even need them. So, thanks, Cal."

The younger man looked like he'd just gotten promoted. "It's my pleasure, sir."

"Christ, Cal. Stop sir-ing me to death. When we're around this bunch of misfits, just call me Archer."

"Thank you, sir!"

Archer just rolled his eyes as he pulled out the last item from the FC unit. When Regent Spartan reached out to grab one of the brownies on the plate, Archer slapped his hand away.

"Hey! Boy, don't make me hit you back. You better be sharing those."

"These are for Serra."

Regent Spartan eyed the small plate of brownies with a frown as Archer walked over to the buffet. He filled Serra's special plate with food, then carried everything back over to the dining room table and set them down while sending a fierce look at Jack Rollins when he caught him eying the brownies, too. "For fuck's sake, there's more brownies in the FC. Get some yourself if you want them. Anyone touches these, and someone will die."

Shaking his head at them, Jax watched as both of his fathers all but lunged towards the FC unit, and shared a smirk with his partner before Archer went back to the buffet to get his own plate of food. Deciding to wait until the others finished foraging through the offerings, Jax headed down the hallway to Serra's office, and held back a sigh as she didn't even look up when he was standing next to her. Takeshi sent him a small smile as he looked up from his own work where he'd been diligently tapping away on the auxiliary unit.

"Go get food."

"I eat when the boss eats."

"It's a wonder you haven't starved to death," Jax muttered, then jerked his head toward the door. "Go grab something. She's eating now."

Takeshi hurried off to try and claim some of the food before everything was consumed. Jax did sigh as Serra ignored their exchange and kept working. He finally gave up and reached out, tilting her head towards him. Amusement flickered as he watched her eyes try to stay focused on the data scrolling on her screen even

138

as he turned her head away from it. She finally gave up, turning those pretty eyes on him.

"Hi."

"Hi. Time to eat."

"Didn't we just do that?"

"About six hours ago."

"Oh. I'm sorry." Her shoulders hunched. "I lost track."

He leaned down, pressing his lips firmly against her. He didn't like her looking like she'd done something wrong just by being who she was. "Stop that now. I'm not going to scold you for losing yourself in your work. Listen to me," Jax said in a hard voice, cutting her off. "I might get annoyed if you aren't taking care of yourself, but that doesn't make you selfish. Between Archer and I, we should be able to remind you. Don't ever compare us to your bitch of a mother."

She sighed, then her mouth firmed as she thought it over. "You're right, she is a bitch."

That made him chuckle. "Sorry, I know I probably shouldn't call her that, but that's how I think of her. This track and trace program is important to all of us, and to be honest, the faster you get this done, the happier I'll be. Let's get these people the hell out of our home," he said, raising his voice.

"We heard that," Cade called out.

Jax winked at Serra, making her laugh. "Come on, let's eat."

Holding onto her hands, he helped her up from her chair and they walked back into the dining room together. Jax pressed a kiss to the top of her head after she sat down next to Archer, then Jax went to get his own food. "Okay, why don't we update each other while we eat," Jax said as he picked up a plate. "No use wasting time, and you can consider your report as payment for eating our food."

Dom snorted in derision, then led off the briefing. "We know that whoever is behind this has to be someone with a connection to Serra, with access to her data unit or travel schedule."

"We took a look through Tania's information. Although everything in me says she could have been behind this, all the information we have gathered points in the negative on that," Cade said. Turning to his daughter he gave her a little sympathetic smile. "Sorry, baby, but after what she did to you, we had to believe she'd be capable of this."

Serra waved off his concern. "It wouldn't surprise me, but I still state she isn't capable of putting this together."

"I agree, but she could be working with someone. She has plenty of credits in her account, but she has basically siphoned all of it straight from you over the years," Jax said, sitting down at the table next to her. His gray eyes frosted over with rage. "That has ended. She'll no longer have access to your accounts, or anything else of yours for that matter."

She nodded as he'd continued to stare at her as if waiting for her to argue. Her mother wouldn't get anything else from her. She had already taken too much. "That is acceptable to me. Thank you for taking care of that."

Jax opened his mouth to scold her for thanking him again, then just sighed, moving on. He barked out a few commands and a transparent screen shimmered into view in mid-air near the table showing several photo IDs and other documents on screen.

Serra felt her heart wrench as she looked at the pictures of all the people closest to her, people she thought of as friends. How many betrayals could she possibly take? There on the screen was a photo of her mother, all six of her guards, her mother's assistant, Eloise, and a secondary assistant Serra used when she was working on a major project, Gavin.

There were also pictures of the Commander that usually flew Serra on his space shuttle when she traveled. He was an older man with a quiet smile who had spent countless nights playing chess with Serra when she couldn't sleep. Then there was his chosen and Second-in-command, a woman who loved showing Serra sneaky moves that could debilitate a man if she needed. There was a shot of her other bonded, the onboard chef who made Serra cookies if she was having a bad day, and the four other crew members that had shared laughs and good times with her over the years. It was likely that one or more of those smiling faces staring out of the screen at her had conspired to steal from her, from the Alliance, and had tried to set her up to take the fall.

Suck it up, Serra told herself. It did no good getting emotional over what was going on. Still, her hand reached over to Sully underneath the table, seeking comfort. When he caught it in his and held it firmly, the connection immediately soothed that ragged part of her that had begun to ache. She needed to be logical, not emotional, she told herself again. More steady now, she forced herself to study the images on the screen with impassive interest.

"I'm surprised you aren't up on the board, too." she said, proud that her voice was steady when she addressed Troy.

A small smile lifted his lips. "I feel sort of left out."

"Takeshi consented to a mind scan and has been cleared completely," Arik said.

"Then why are Officers Meyers and Rhine up there? I thought they'd also been cleared."

"They are, and have agreed to stay under wraps until we need them for the takedown," High Commander Newgate informed her. "They still have a part to play in this, so we're leaving them up on the board. Same goes with your flight crew. Since you aren't scheduled to meet up with them until after the sale in New Vega, it lowers them down the list."

Takeshi studied the board. "Gavin worked with us on the stealth project."

Serra shook her head. "He did, but only on small parts of it, and he hasn't been around for months now. One of his fathers is sick and he's been on leave."

"But he worked on the project and had knowledge and access, which means he stays a person of interested until we have proof he's not a part of this," Dom added.

"My gut says it's one or more of the guards, so we've been taking a hard look at the four that aren't in custody," Jax said.

"I've been looking at Officer Rick Harding," Andrew informed them. "Digging into his data confirms he is what he seems on the surface. A solid officer, who likes to travel when he's on duty, and spends time with his family on X4 whenever he isn't on the roll."

"Same goes for his partner, Officer Diego Ramirez, except for the family ties," Jack said.

"He was a lone wolf until he paired up with Harding. My sources say they are courting a woman on X4," Archer added after he finished chewing a bite of his sandwich. "I think they will be putting in for a transfer as soon as they work up the courage to ask her to be their chosen."

"You mean some men ask?" Amusement sparkled in Serra's eyes as she smiled at him.

"If we had asked, you might have said no," Archer said before leaning in to kiss her.

"There is no kissing during a briefing!" Dom snapped. Archer sent him a pitying glance before Dom switched the topic back to intergalactic conspiracies and treason. "What we've found on Officers Nolan and Prentice has my bell ringing. They're fucking dirty."

"Charles Nolan has a gambling problem, and was under for almost sixty thousand two years ago on New Vega," Jax said, speaking of the large, impressive vessel that traveled around space. New Vega catered to all types of clientele, all looking for the same thing...pleasure. Whether it be gambling, sex, or other entertainment, New Vega offered it, for a price. "One week later, the marker was paid off in full. Timing coincides with a sale of the shield tech we discovered later when a Sentinel seized a marauding vessel in Alliance territory."

"They put up resistance, but the shielding didn't hold against the Alliance Sentinel's firepower," Cade added. "When they were boarded, they had the stolen tech uploaded and installed onboard. That incident was six months after the sale."

"I remember that," Serra said. "Whoever is buying the shield tech on the black market doesn't understand that if it isn't installed properly, it begins to break down….becomes ineffective over time. We built in that failsafe in case something like this happened."

Takeshi grinned at her. "Your idea. And it was a brilliant one at that."

"I only thought of it because you suggested it," Serra argued.

A dark frown settled over Regent Spartan's face. "Why wasn't I told about this failsafe?"

"Regent Kobe knows, as he is my liaison with the council. Only the people on the install team knew about the failsafe. I believe Regent Kobe thought it was safer that way."

"Damn bastard. He's been quiet about it, and convinced the council to downgrade the threat level since we've discovered the shield tech on unauthorized vessels. We thought someone was cloning the tech, but this makes more sense now. He and I are going to be having words soon. Very soon," Regent Spartan repeated ominously.

"We became aware of this problem when we discovered that a D'Aire traitor had purchased the shielding through improper means. He was questioned after he and his men attacked another ship, but he refused to give us the name of his contact," Arik said, almost pleasantly.

"Can we question him?" Roman Newgate demanded.

"He is no longer living. D'Aire justice is swift and exacting."

"I'll say," Cade muttered, then raised his voice to address everyone. "Nolan still spends most of his time off duty on New Vega."

"Not just Nolan. Jacob Prentice is into this up to his neck, too," Dom remarked. "Whenever Nolan is gambling, Prentice goes with him, but he tends to spend most of his time at the sex clubs. He prefers real to sex droids."

"That would take a lot of money. The places on New Vega aren't cheap. Or so I've heard," Jack added quickly.

"More money than he has. His accounts don't have enough to cover his spending habits, so he has to have one hidden somewhere."

"They both have lines of credit on New Vega, with more than they make from their positions, but not enough to cover what they'd be making from the sales. Could they have someone working with them on New Vega?"

Dom shook his head. "I know the Krytos who own New Vega. They may make their money dealing with vices of all kinds, but they wouldn't allow something like this. They may skirt the lines of regulations, but they'd never cross it. Not this far. When the Krytos made the pact with the Alliance, they took it very seriously. Anyone found going against our laws would be considered the worse sort of betrayer."

"They would personally rip anyone into pieces if they discovered someone dealing black market goods aboard their vessel," Arik added. "We've seen them in action. If you think D'Aire justice is harsh, Krytos justice is even more brutal."

Archer frowned. "Something isn't playing right for me. These two assholes were too easy to find. If they are in charge of this, don't you think they would have done a better job hiding it?"

"It hasn't exactly been easy," Regent Spartan pointed out. "It's taken all of us, and we still haven't found their hidden accounts. We have no actual proof."

"We will. I'm sure of that. But I get what you mean," Dom agreed grudgingly. "These two are too fucking stupid to run a scheme like this. I see them as a blind. Someone to take the fall for the real person in charge."

"But who then?" Serra asked. "There isn't anyone else who has access and the knowhow to pull this off."

"I think there is," Cal said quietly. All eyes turned to Officer Cal Ryans, making him fidget in his seat.

144

"Explain."

Cal cleared his throat that had suddenly gone as dry as the badlands. "You've overlooked the one person up there that has both the access and a foundation in electronics."

Serra followed his gaze back to the board, where he was looking at the smiling face of Eloise Greer, her mother's assistant. She battled back her first instinctive denial, and thought it through. Eloise had come to her three years ago as a potential assistant for her own work. Even though she had a basic knowledge of electronics, Eloise hadn't been able to grasp the work fast enough for Serra to continue using her. Eloise had seemed happy enough staying with them as Tania's assistant, enjoying the travel and exposure to other cultures.

It all made a terrible kind of sense.

"I think Cal is right," she said softly. "She's around enough to know what I've been working on and has the access to my mother's accounts since Eloise pays her bills."

"Which means she's had access to yours." Jax's jaw clenched.

"Yes. I found she lacked the skills to be useful as my own assistant, but she'd know enough to put that block on my unit. I don't think she would be capable of creating it, but she'd know enough to install it."

"And maybe by installing it, she got a look at the data you had on your unit and thought about how she could profit from it," Archer said thoughtfully.

"This is good. Let's dig into this woman's life. Accounts, contacts, the works." Jax turned fierce eyes on Officer Cal Ryans. "Damn good work, Cal."

"Thank you, sir!"

"If it's her, we'll take her down." Jax turned to Serra. "How close are you to finishing that program?"

"I think we almost have it. This was a good place to stop, actually. I need to think a few things over before we run a sim on the cloned unit."

"We need to make sure we don't ping any security on the end-user's unit when they upload the altered schematics we tag." Takeshi agreed after he swallowed a bite of his sandwich. "What if we put some sort of timer on the tag so that it doesn't activate until the unit idles—"

"No, I've got it set so it burrows deep upon upload," Serra responded.

"I think my eyes just glazed over," Dom said to no one in particular.

"We don't need to understand what they're talking about, as long as they do," Andrew said, patting Dom on the shoulder.

"Sorry. Basically, yes. We'll be ready to run the tests later."

"You mean tomorrow," Archer said. "We have the gala tonight."

Serra barely held back a groan. How could she have forgotten about that? She had to bite her lip to hold back her apology, but sensed that Jax and Sully knew what she was thinking by the way they were looking at her. She'd gotten so used to apologizing for her behavior over the years that it was a knee-jerk reaction now whenever she forgot something because of her work.

Her mother had been the ultimate at laying on the heavy guilt trip whenever Serra screwed up. She'd gotten used to hearing how selfish she was to make her mother drop everything to make sure Serra ate or slept. Serra knew she often lost herself in her projects, and had tried changing that, but it was no use. At least Jax and Sully didn't seem too bothered by it.

"We can do the tests tomorrow," she said after taking a sip of her coffee. "I'll have to start getting ready soon anyways."

"I am always fascinated by the female rituals one goes through before an event," Arik said.

"And you'll keep wondering until you find your keeper," Jax warned.

Arik smiled in response. Amused, Serra watched their exchange, then was distracted as her wrist unit beeped. She looked

146

down at the data scrolling on the screen and smiled. "Ah. Troy, I forgot to tell you. I signed a licensing agreement for the nano-cleanser with G-Mex Robotics. You should be getting…there it is."

Takeshi looked at his own wrist unit, checking the message, then the usually taciturn man's eyes widened comically. "Holy shit! What the hell is this?"

"That's your half of the sale. We should also be receiving royalty percentages each month from now on. I think I got us a pretty good deal. I may not particularly care for the owners of the company, but they do have good market shares."

"I can't accept this. I only tweaked some of the code—"

Serra held up a hand. "I told you, if I took the concept to the private sector I would split it with you. You helped me complete the project, so you deserve half."

"I could retire on this now," he whispered with a baffled laugh.

"I really hope you won't," Serra said, honestly. "I sincerely enjoy working with you, and hope to continue doing so well into the future."

"I wouldn't give up my position for worlds," Takeshi swore with fervor. "Plus, I love the travel and all the places we get to go to."

"Guess you're going to miss that now," Jax said absently as he continued to eat.

Serra paused with her sandwich in her hand. She slowly lowered it back to her plate, staring at him. "Miss what?"

"The traveling. It's not like you can bounce around planets now that we're a bonded unit. You belong here with me and Archer now, not gallivanting around space."

Temper flashed bright and hot inside of her, obliterating everything else that she had been thinking about. Who the hell did he think he was making that decision for her without even discussing it? Turning to Sully, she asked, "Is that how you both feel?"

Archer opened his mouth to respond, but seeing the fury on her face had him pausing. That seemed enough to set her off, though.

"How dare you," she said softly. Finally sensing her anger, Jax finally turned and looked at her, and the surprise on his face made her want to smack him.

"You're angry."

"You think? You have no right to dictate to me like your word is law as to whether or not I continue my work. Just because you're the commander of the Capital, that doesn't make your job more important than mine. You may run this city, but you don't run me, not even as my bonded."

"Serra, listen—"

"No, you listen," she said, rising to her feet. "What I do isn't just gallivanting around the damn universe. I might not hold your rank, but what I do saves lives."

"He didn't mean—"

She rounded on Sully, burning him with the heat of her rage as well. "Don't you defend him. What he said was clear enough. Both of you just assumed that you would go on with your own duties, without a single thought for what that would mean to me and the work I do. Perhaps you should have considered this before you claimed me. Now, I have a gala to get ready for and I would like to do so alone." With that, she stomped off, leaving the room as she muttered about the stupidity of men.

"Stupid," Cade said in agreement, once she was gone. "You two are dumb as rocks."

"Hell, I'm not even bonded and I know better," Dom retorted with a shake of his head. "That was fucking painful to watch."

"What the fuck?" Jax exploded, on the defensive now. He could feel shame curl in his gut, and that only made him more furious. "It's not like we haven't had to adjust our lives as well. This isn't easy for any of us, but what the hell are we supposed to do? We can't just leave the Capital for months at a time."

"But we just assumed she would stay here with us," Archer explained. "It's not enough that we fixed up our suite to suit her. What she does saves lives, and we never even considered that."

"Not just for the Alliance," Arik added softly. "What she does ensures the safety of all our worlds."

"Fuck."

Regent Spartan sent his son a sympathetic glance. "Don't worry. Over the years to come you'll get used to it. I'm sure you'll get plenty of practice."

Jax glared at him. "Get used to what?"

"Groveling. I'd say you have some pretty fucking epic groveling to do."

Chapter Eleven

The tension was so thick it could be cut with a blade.

Serra stared out of the window of their vehicle as they headed toward the Hall of Regents, where the Freedom Day Gala was taking place. She completely ignored the two men watching her with cautious eyes, like she was a bomb that was about to go off at any moment. She'd asked them not to speak to her until she had better control of her anger, and was grateful when they'd complied. She was still exceptionally irritated with both her bonded, although her ire had lessened a fraction since that afternoon.

She'd taken her time getting ready for the event, using the distance from Jax and Sully to consider exactly what she wanted to say to them. In truth, they each had a vital role to play within the Alliance. She had been blind to the consequences of her claiming, so focused on the joy of being with them again that she hadn't thought about what it meant for their future. It had probably been the same for the men, but that still didn't excuse their assumptions that she would be the one to give up her travels just because they declared it.

Her work—at least the creation part of it—could be done anywhere, and she'd be happy to move her lab and headquarters to the Capital to be with them. But she would still need to travel. No, it wasn't just a need…she loved the quiet of space, the rush of being able to visit different planets and interact with other races.

However, the reality was that this decision was bigger than just what her preference was.

Serra was tasked with protecting millions of lives, not only within the Alliance territories spread throughout the universe, but also the races that Earth called allies. No one knew her creations the way she did, and it wasn't something she could train someone to do. The shield components changed when it was merged with whatever system it was installed in, meaning each mainframe had to be calibrated differently.

She'd never forgive herself if someone was hurt because she didn't do her job.

"Serra, this is killing me. You have to talk to us, damn it!"

Somehow she knew Jax would be the one to break first. He was an action man, and the silence had to have been setting his teeth on edge. Serra finally turned to look at her bonded. Jax and Sully both looked mighty tasty dressed all in black in their dress uniforms, the only color were the metal bars on their collars signifying their rank as commanders.

She was new to having a relationship, and having one with two men was even more confusing, but there was some comfort in knowing that she still wanted them even though she was pissed. Both men were looking at her with a mixture of anger and sadness. The anger she could deal with, but their sadness affected her. "I'm still angry with you."

"We understand that, but nothing will get better if we don't talk about this," Archer pressed.

"True, but my question is this then. Can we talk about this, or will it just be the two of you telling me that you've already decided how things are going to be." She held up a hand to stop them from speaking. "I understand that you've integrated me into your lives, and I appreciate all the changes you've made to help me adapt, but this isn't something you can just dictate, then declare everything is settled."

"We didn't mean to do that, and I know it came out that way," Jax hurried to explain. "What you want is important to us, Serra. We didn't enslave you when we claimed you."

"We'll work this out. That's a promise," Archer said.

The conversation was put on hold when the vehicle came to a stop in front of the Hall of Regents. Archer got out first, then Jax, who turned to help Serra out. She took his arm and Archer's as they

152

walked toward the building, filing into the crowd of people also heading inside.

There was a sense of pride that filled Serra when she noticed how many people wanted Jax and Sully's attention, and the respectful way other elites treated them. The Freedom Day Gala was the event of the season, and anyone who was anyone attended. The usually austere interior of the hall had been decorated in honor of Freedom Day with streams of red material and banners highlighting the red and black symbol of the United Federation Command Alliance. Large banners with the Dragon Warrior, D'Aire and Krytos emblems also hung as tribute to the allies that helped Earth defeat the Zyphir.

High command elites and their families mingled with D'Aire, Krytos and visiting dignitaries from other worlds, and elaborate chandeliers created soft spotlights on all the magnificently dressed individuals filling the hall. Most of the elites wore the black dress uniforms, but women wore gowns in every color imaginable.

Once inside the main hall, Serra turned to give Sully her back so he could remove her cloak, and heard the harsh breath both he and Jax sucked in when her dress was revealed. The gown she had chosen to wear was a halter style that left her back completely bare, made of a dark crimson fabric that looked like shiny, wet plastic, but was as soft as silk. The dress showed off her tattooed arm, the deep red highlighting the mercurial black lines on her skin. The plunging neckline ended in a deep V between her breasts, and the small heart necklace made of *xithradite* Sully had given her was her only adornment.

Tonight she had decided to make her own sort of statement as this was their first official outing since they had claimed her. She wanted everyone to see that together, they were a united force...a powerful force that represented the Alliance.

"Holy god," Jax breathed out reverently as he looked at her. A tingle of excitement whipping through her blood stream as his eyes went to molten silver, searing through her with his heated stare.

153

Archer reached out a hand, stroking it over her hip as if to see if the fabric was as slick as it looked. "You look like a wet dream."

She smiled, pleased with their reactions, then had to hold back her laughter as Jax growled at a group of elites that were eying her in appreciation. The flash of jealousy she saw in his dark eyes had an answering lust curling in her belly. The soldiers snapped to attention and quickly fled the area, a few of them even breaking out into a slight run to get away from Jax's wrath.

"Ah, there you are," High Commander Newgate said as he joined them. "Serra, you look absolutely ravishing." She thanked him, then shook her head as both Jax and Sully maneuvered their bodies to block her from view. Roman Newgate coughed to cover his laugh. "Commander Archer. I'm sorry to pull you away from your chosen, but there is something that needs your attention."

"Of course there is," Archer said with a sigh. Leaning down, he pressed a kiss against Serra's lip. "I'll be back as soon as I can."

"All right." She was going to suggest she and Jax get something to drink after they left, but was distracted when Jax gripped her hand in his and began pulling her through the crowd. "Jax, what are you doing?"

"We need to finish our conversation, and we can't do it in here when all I want to do is punch every fucking man staring at you."

She didn't know whether to be pleased or annoyed by the way he dragged her out onto one of the terraces, into the cool night air. Jax started to move to the left, but quickly turned the other way as they heard voices coming from a group of people that had also escaped the crowd inside. She let him pull her into a dark corner at the far end of the terrace, behind a row of potted plants that shielded them from view.

Excitement whipped through her when her back hit the smooth surface of the wall as he pressed her back into the shadows against the side of the building. It felt like they were in their own little world even though the faint sound of voices and laughter from the other people on the balcony danced lightly on the breeze.

154

Serra was unsurprised by his caveman behavior. Jax always reminded her of a wild beast. He held that part of himself under tight control most of the time, but it was always there, just beneath the surface. She watched a myriad of expressions flicker over his face as she waited for him to speak, and simply admired the sharp angles of his handsome face in the silence. There was an intensity about him that excited her, but she couldn't give into her desire.

Not yet.

Anger, confusion, lust and a healthy dose of regret warred inside of Jax as he stared down at Serra. Cast in shadows, her beautiful face looked even more arresting. He hated knowing she was angry with him, no matter how much he deserved her ire. She made him feel…too much, and those unfamiliar emotions had him riding the thin edge of his control.

Earlier, he had wanted to go after her when she'd left the room, to try and explain why they had to stay in the Capital. When he'd become the commander of the Capital, he'd taken an oath, made a commitment that he had never faltered to execute to the best of his abilities.

But that had been before claiming Serra.

He was glad he'd heeded the advice of the other men, and given Serra the space she had asked for. Needing time to think himself, Jax had retreated to the gym on the lower level so he could work off some of his own anger and frustration. After a few minutes of hitting the bags, Jax felt his annoyance dissipate under the weight of his shame. So what that they had changed the colors of the suite or reminded her to eat a few meals? They'd fucking claimed her while she had been passed out, and at what cost? She had been free to choose for herself, and they had taken that choice away from her.

She loved them, he knew it. Just as he knew they could make her happy, but not if they asked her to give up her purpose and her pride. When he'd finished his workout, he'd turned to see Archer sitting on the bench, waiting for him. Together, they discussed what Jax had figured out while he had been working out.

Nothing mattered more than Serra.

Jax knew that the gala wasn't the right place to discuss this, but he couldn't stand the distance between them any longer. "Fuck. I'm sorry, Serra."

Shit, he didn't mean to just blurt it out like that, but when she looked up at him like that, with those gorgeous green eyes so bright and clear, he lost his fucking mind. She was so fucking precious to him. Her lips twitched, and he felt some of his tension ease. He could deal with her amusement better than her disappointment. And she had been disappointed in him. In both him and Archer, but the majority of the blame rested on Jax's shoulders.

"I need more data to decide whether or not that constitutes a forgivable declaration of contrition. What exactly are you apologizing for again?"

Damn it. It wasn't fair for her to look so fucking sexy while putting him in his place. His eyes narrowed. "I'm sorry for being an ass."

One of her brows lifted. "That's still not telling me much, Jax."

That startled a laugh out of him. Lowering his head, he rested his brow against hers, needing that connection to her. "I'm sorry for what I said earlier. I don't think my position is more important than yours. You save lives, Serra. What could be more essential than that?"

"You're a leader, Jax. I know the people in the Capital need you—"

Jax lifted a finger and pressed it to her lips to stop her from continuing. "They may need me, but no one is more important to me than you. We'll work something out. If you're willing to remain in the Capital most of the time and use it as a base of operations, then Archer and I will trade off going with you when you travel."

She opened her mouth, then closed it again. As ungrateful as it sounded, she wanted both of her men with her when she traveled, not just one. She nodded slowly as she considered what he'd said. "It isn't the best situation, but it's a starting point. I have to

156

apologize as well. I shouldn't have just left earlier. I should have stayed so we could discuss it, but sometimes I do better when I have some time to process what's happening before I respond."

"I understand, sweetheart. This is new to all of us, including Archer." He brushed his lips lightly over hers. "Am I forgiven?"

"Yes. I have it on good authority that men have stupid moments that need to be forgiven often."

Jax pulled back to frown down at her. "And who told you that?"

"I spoke to Alexis earlier." She shrugged. "She's my only friend that is bonded...or mated, in her case. I don't know how she handles four mates. It's difficult enough with the two of you, if I had two more of you, I think I'd end up killing someone."

"You only need two of us to keep you busy," Jax growled. He kissed her harder this time, let the heat seep through so they were both breathing hard when he pulled back. "Come on. We have to get the hell out of here before I take you against this wall."

He started to move, but she jerked at the jacket of his uniform, holding him in place. "We could do it...out here?"

He went hard as stone hearing the intrigue in her voice, and groaned. "Serra, you can't say shit like that to me."

"Like what? You're the one who brought it up."

When she tried to push past him, he shoved her back against the wall. Her eyes widened as he pressed closer, allowing her to feel his steel-hard cock against her stomach.

"Do you feel that?" he demanded. "Push me a little more and I'll be inside you. Right here, right now. Understand?"

She tilted her head, looking up at him thoughtfully. "Why are you angry?"

His steel-gray eyes softened instantly, and his hand lifted to cup her cheek. "I'm not angry at you, but damn do you push my control. Do you think I want to take you out here, where anyone can walk over and see us?"

Serra looked away to survey their surroundings, then her eyes met his again. Lowering her voice, she whispered, "I don't think anyone can see us."

"Son of a bitch…"

Jax captured her mouth, thrusting his tongue deep as he fed off her. He felt her arms wrap around his neck as their tongues tangled together…stroking, tasting. "We've been careful with you," he murmured before nipping lightly at her lower lip. "But there's a part of you that wants to be wild, isn't there? You want to see just how far you can push me…want to see what I'll do when I lose control. You want to feel that rush of being taken."

"Jax…"

She let out a gasp when his hand wrapped around her throat, tilting her head back. "Answer me. Tell me what you want."

"I want it all. You're my bonded, don't hold back on me. Give it to me, give me all you've got," she challenged.

Jax felt his cock throbbing, urging him on to take what she offered. What she demanded of him. He could see the hunger in her eyes, could feel the need pulsing through her veins beneath his palm. He felt the thrill of being wanted, of having her need him as he needed her. He watched her as his other hand dropped down to her thigh, slowly lifting the hem of her dress.

"I'm going to take you," he promised darkly, pressing the full length of his powerful body against her. "I'll take you, and I won't stop until you're full of me. It's going to be fast, hard and a little rough, but you'll love it, won't you, sweetheart?"

"Yes," she panted out. "God, yes. Please—"

Her cry was cut off as his mouth crushed down on hers again, feeding that desperate hunger inside of him. He felt his control snap, like a thin thread that held back the madness of his need for her, and let the fires of lust consumed them both.

Serra moaned as he shoved her roughly against the wall. He felt vicious triumph rip through him when she clung to his arms, her nails biting through the fabric of his uniform jacket. He shoved the skirt of her dress all the way up, exposing her to the cool night air, and let out a frustrated growl as his fingers brushed over the barrier of her panties. He needed to feel the slick flesh of her pussy with nothing between them.

Swept away in the storm of passion raging between them, he grabbed hold of the thin material and jerked hard, tearing the panties from her body, dropping them carelessly to the floor. Touching her was electric, and he felt the jolt sing up his arm as his hand met the heated flesh of her pussy, hot and slick as he slid two of his fingers inside her. He felt her tremble and knew he she was ready for him.

"Oh, God!"

Serra's head fell back against the wall. His touch was like magic, making her body hum with pleasure. He muffled the sound of her moans with his own mouth when his thumb played over her clit, watching her with predatory eyes that gave her no doubt how much he wanted her.

She heard his zipper releasing, then felt his cock touching her bare skin. Lifting her easily, he braced her back against the wall with his large body pressing tight against her front. "Wrap your legs around me," he demanded in a harsh whisper. "Do it now."

Eagerly, she did as he asked, then felt the broad head of his cock pressing against her entrance of her pussy. Mouth crushing down on hers again, he drank down her cry of pleasure as he thrust hard, filling her with the full length of his cock.

It was madness.

There in the shadows, their eyes met and held. So much was said without saying a word, with only the sound of their ragged breathing breaking through the silence. She watched the beads of sweat trickling down his forehead, and lifted her hands from his shoulders to wipe them away before they dripped into his eyes. Sounds from the gala drifted on the wind, adding a little sense of fear into the mix at the thought of strangers catching them.

But nothing could stop them now.

The cool night breeze created a stimulating contrast to their heated bodies. The contrasting sensations drove her closer toward the edge of release, and he pushed her even further when he shifted his hips. Her body jerked when his pelvis hit her clit, his every thrust slapping that tight bundle of nerves as he fucked her.

"Jax. Oh, God, Jax—"

"Shh, quiet now. You don't want us to get caught, do you? If any other man saw you like this I'd have to kill him. You're mine," Jax snarled as his hips pumped, thrusting his cock into her hard and fast, just like he'd promised.

"Jax, I'm going to come…" she warned on a breathless whisper.

"Do it. Come on my cock and take me with you. Give it to me. Milk my seed from me when you come."

Jerking forward, she muffled her scream against his bare throat as she gave herself over to the pleasure. She bit down hard when he pushed her that final inch so her body shuddered as she came. Legs tensed around his waist, gripping him tight as the ripples of her climax tore through her. She felt the deep guttural growl rumble in his chest as he came, following her over the edge as he filled her with pulse after pulse of his hot cum.

Jax felt his legs shaking, and had to brace a hand against the wall so he wouldn't crush Serra as he slumped forward. Now that the storm of passion was over, he gentled his touch, pressing soft kisses on her cheek as she rested her head on his shoulder.

"So…would that be considered a quickie?"

He snorted in amusement as he tried to catch his breath. "Was that a complaint?"

"Not at all. I was just wondering, since a quickie was on my list of things to do."

Shifting, he looked at her in astonishment. "You have a list?"

"Of course I do."

"What exactly is on this list?"

She sighed happily. "You'll just have to wait and see."

160

Chapter Twelve

Serra detoured to the restroom to clean up before heading back into the main hall where her men waited for her. She exchanged smiles with several guests as she moved through the crowd. She felt lighter. Sated from her excursion with Jax, yes, but also centered. It eased her mind to know that they were willing to compromise and work something out so she wouldn't have to give up her work. Both Jax and Sully were alpha to the core, but she understood now that they would always pay attention to what mattered to her.

"Serra."

Distracted by her own thoughts, Serra missed the approach of her fathers' mistress, Diane Delacourt. The Delacourt family was a powerful force within the Alliance. Serra had once felt sorry for Diane after learning how she had fallen in love with her fathers as a young woman, but since she was infertile, she hadn't been a suitable candidate for their chosen. Diane was polished, sophisticated and stunningly beautiful, but Serra had never liked her.

"I thought that was you, Serra," Diane said, coming to a stop in front of Serra. The older woman pressed air kisses near Serra's cheeks before stepping back to smile. "How nice to see you. And, my, don't you look...nice tonight."

Serra heard the not so subtle dig on her daring crimson gown. Dressed in a conservative gown of midnight blue, Serra looked at the abundance of sapphires draped over Diane's neck, wrists and fingers with her own not so subtle look of disgust.

"Diane. You certainly look...sparkling."

"Cade and Andrew tell me congratulations are in order." Diane cast a quick glance at the claiming mark near Serra's eyes. For a moment the other woman's smile turned brittle before it smoothed back into her usual polite mask. "It is quite an accomplishment to have attached yourself to two strong elites such as Commander

Spartan and Commander Archer. I'm sure they're a great comfort to you."

"What do you mean?"

Diane shot her a sympathetic look that instantly put Serra on alert. "I know Cade and Andrew attended your claiming ceremony. I just wanted to tell you how brave I think you are for handling all of this so well."

"Brave? I don't understand what you're getting at."

Diane reached out and patted Serra's hand, making her want to snatch it away from the older woman's touch. Serra knew Diane was lying, but didn't understand why. Both of her fathers had told everyone that they were on a special assignment, even Diane, and they had been careful not to talk to anyone since, due to the operation they were all involved in. Sure, it was possible that Diane had found out from one of the guests that had attended ceremony. They had always known word would get out, but why would Diane lie about it?

Diane sighed. "This must all be so difficult for you. It's not like Cade or Andrew could say no when ordered to attend an event by their commanders."

Serra's eyes narrowed as her temper began to spike. "They weren't ordered to attend. And Jax and Sully aren't my fathers' commanders. They're generals in Light City, not the Capital."

"Still," Diane waved that away with a careless gesture that had the sapphires on her wrist flashing in the light. "You bonded with two powerful Alliance commanders. Of course they couldn't say no, even though you know how they really feel about you. I know about the letter they sent you, asking you not to come visit us. This must be so hard for you to see them again after everything that has happened."

Serra's mind raced even as she struggled to hide her rage. "How do you know about that letter, Diane?" she asked, trying for a curious expression.

"I begged them not to send it," Diane whispered in a voice filled with sympathy. "I told them that it was cruel, but they thought it was best you understood how they felt. They never wanted a daughter. Not really. But how can they say that to you now that you're bonded to Commander Spartan and Archer?"

"That's odd. Considering that I know that letter wasn't real. My fathers never sent it." Serra voice went hard, and she watched as Diane's face paled. "So I'll ask again, how do you know about the letter?"

"That's a damn good question," Donna Spartan-Rollins snapped from behind them. Serra turned around as saw Jax's mother glaring at Diane with such disgust it was a wonder the other woman didn't wither under the weight of it.

"Donna, there's been some sort of misunderstanding—"

"I don't think you can call what you just said a misunderstanding. Serra, dear," Donna said, never looking away from Diane. "Why don't you go get your men while I keep Diane here. I suggest you stay right where you are, or I'd be happy to knock you on your lying, gaudy ass."

Serra spun around, intent to do just that, but she saw that Jax and Sully were already pushing through the crowd. Jax reached her first and gripped her arms so tight she had to hold back a wince. "What is it? What's wrong?"

She filled them in, and saw the fury on her fathers faces as they joined them. Cade whirled on Diane, who tried to step back from his wrath only to bump into Dom who had moved in behind her. "You sent that letter? How could you, Diane?" Cade roared.

"I did it for you, Cade!" she pleaded. "I love you and Andrew. Tania said—"

"Tania," Andrew muttered in revulsion. "That bloody bitch is a plague."

"I'm taking Ms. Delacourt into custody," Dom informed them as he restrained the now weeping woman.

"I'll come with you. I want to hear what she has to say," Jax said, his voice filled with icy distain. Those gray eyes warmed as he looked down at Serra. "Did you want to come?"

"Is it all right if I just stay here?"

"I'll stay," Archer offered, wrapping an arm around her waist, drawing her close. Gratefully, she burrowed into his side. Jax kissed her lightly then walked off with Dom, the crowd parting as they escorted the wailing woman out of the hall.

Ignoring the onlookers in the crowd, Cade turned to Serra with devastated eyes. "I'm so sorry, baby."

"We should go with them. We have to know the extent of the damage she's done," Andrew clarified, his own voice broken. "Serra—"

"Stop," Serra commanded. Over the last week, she had spent a lot of time with her fathers, getting to know them again. They weren't perfect, and they had made mistakes in the past, but they were healing together, and that was all that mattered to her. "This isn't your fault. Anything she's done isn't on you."

"She'll be taken care of," Regent Spartan said as he and Jack walked up to join them. Donna leaned into Jack's side as Ian Spartan cupped her face. "Will you forgive me if I leave for a little while?"

"Go." Donna smiled. "I never did like her. She's an…obvious sort of woman."

"Not obvious to us, apparently," Cade said bitterly.

"You have a penis. Pretty faces tend to get in the way of your kind seeing the true nature of a woman sometimes."

"Darling," Jack murmured into Donna's ear. "I happen to be very fond of your pretty face."

"Yes, but I've never hidden who I really am with you."

"No, you tend to speak your mind quite clearly," Ian Spartan said with a laugh. He leaned down to place a tender kiss on her lips. "I will try to get back to you soon."

"I'll be waiting." The regent left with Serra's fathers, and Donna smiled brightly at Serra. "Well, you sure know how to spice up a party."

Serra choked back a laugh. "That was unintentional on my part."

Archer pressed his lips to her forehead as he reached down to still her fingers tapping against her thigh with his hand. "I'm sorry, hummingbird."

She took a deep breath, then let it out slowly. "They'll figure out what to do with her. I'm just glad she won't be influencing my relationship with my fathers anymore."

"She won't," Archer agreed, then turned to address the older couple. "Now, if you would excuse us, I still haven't gotten the chance to dance with my woman."

He led Serra onto the dance floor, sweeping her into his arms. "The hits just keep on coming, don't they? I'm sorry for upsetting you earlier, Serra."

"It's okay. I think we still have a lot to learn about making this relationship work."

"But we will, I swear it."

She smiled up at him. "You know, Jax apologized…thoroughly outside."

"I heard," Archer lowered his voice to a seductive whisper as lust whipped through his system, heating his blood. "Perhaps I should also apologize…in private as well."

"Perhaps you should," she said with a laugh.

"Then I will, in great detail."

He took her hand and pulled her off of the dance floor. And she was still laughing when he found a private room and followed through with his promise.

"Download is complete. They took the bait."

Archer looked over at Serra as she sat back in her chair with a pleased look on her face. They were in the conference room on the space cruiser taking them to New Vega, having just left the testing site right outside of Light City. The stealth tech had been a wonder to see, and Archer had been filled with pride at witnessing what his woman had created.

After the gala, Archer and Serra had met Jax back at their quarters. The men had interrogated Diane thoroughly, and found that she was nothing more than a silly, sad woman who had used an opportunity presented to her to keep Cade and Andrew all to herself. Shortly after Diane had started seeing them, Tania had contacted her to let her know that she didn't mind the other woman being with her bonded, as long as Diane did what she could to keep them away from Serra. Since Diane knew that Serra didn't like her, she'd agreed.

Diane Delacourt's life was over now, or at least the lavish lifestyle she was used to. She was being kept in custody until the mission was complete, so she'd have no chance to contact Tania to warn her about what was going on. But after this was over, she'd be freed. What she did was petty and malicious, but she hadn't broken any law. They'd make damn sure she paid for her actions, and Archer had a feeling living in disgrace and being a social pariah would be just as bad as being put in prison.

Moving ahead with the plan, Jax and Archer had accompanied Serra to Light City for the testing of the stealth tech. The tests had gone well, and Serra only had to make a few corrections before she had signed off on the final schematics. When she'd gotten her copy, Serra stored the finalized plans onto a secured data unit she had personally modified for her use, with new security features that practically made it impossible for anyone to even power the damn thing on. She uploaded the altered schematics onto her old unit so whoever had the hidden link on it would be able to access it. She'd attached the track and trace program to the file, and whoever was behind the theft had taken the bait.

Now, it was only a matter of tracking the file to see who the buyer was.

They had a full entourage on this trip, which annoyed Archer despite knowing it was necessary. In addition to their trio, Serra's fathers, Dom, Arik, Takeshi, Skylar, High Commander Newgate, and Officers Ryans, Meyer and Rhine had come along on for the ride. Archer and Jax had spread the word that they were taking this trip in celebration of him and Jax claiming Serra, but in reality this op would hopefully end the threat against the Alliance and shut down a black market menace that had been plaguing them for months.

Jax, Dom, Andrew, High Commander Newgate and the officers had escaped to the onboard gym to work away the stress of being confined within the cruiser. Jax had always hated being tethered to one place for too long, just as much as he hated the constant barrage of people vying for his attention when they were on duty.

Archer dealt with the monotonous strains of leadership better than Jax, but that was only because he hid his impatience better. The confinement was getting to him as well, and he needed to get the hell out of there for a while, but he had a different kind of workout in mind.

"So, now we wait and see who this fucker sells it to, right?" Skylar asked, ignoring the large D'Aire male staring at her, just as she had been for the last hour or so.

"That's right." Serra looked down at her screen again, trying to ignore the building tension in the room. "We just have to wait and see. And I'm trying to get a location for the thief, but their unit is blocked."

Since they had boarded the cruiser, Serra had sensed something going on between Skylar, Dom and Arik, but she didn't ask about it. She wasn't sure she really wanted to know. Dom and Skylar couldn't seem to have a conversation without sniping at each other, while Arik spent most of his time staring at Skylar in silence.

Serra could tell both men were getting on her friend's nerves, and she only hoped that Skylar didn't end up punching the D'Aire ambassador or shocking her director unconscious if he thought to try to add some more sex into his life, like Serra had suggested.

She was glad that Skylar had been assigned as her personal bodyguard for the trip. Her friend had been thrilled by the free trip to New Vega, but sobered when she had been read into the facts of the op they'd put together. Still, with all the men involved, it was nice to have another woman around, even if that woman was more volatile than the rest of them put together.

"It's a good plan." Cade patted her arm. "Why don't you take a break now? We've got two more days until we dock on New Vega. You can't just keep staring at your data screen."

"Oh, but…"

"Go. I can keep watch and tag you if something happens," Takeshi said, not bothering to look up from his own screen.

"If you can pull yourself away from Galaxy Invaders," Cade grumbled.

Takeshi's shoulders hunched. "This game helps my coordination and its fucking fun, so lay off."

"Sure…what level are you on?"

"Four eighty six."

"Bullshit!"

Amused, Skylar watched Cade and Takeshi fight for control of the game. "For god's sake, put the game on the big screen. I'm gonna go take a nap," Skylar announced as she stood up. The doors automatically opened as she strode toward them, then closed again after she left.

"She has such pain inside her," Arik said softly as Takeshi and Cade turned their attention to transferring the game onto the wall screen.

Archer and Serra shared a speaking glance, then they both looked back at Arik. "I don't think you want to set your sights there, friend," Archer warned.

"I find her intriguing."

"Sure you do," Serra said carefully. "But I'm not sure the interest is reciprocated."

"Oh, it is," Arik countered with a slow grin. "She just won't admit it…yet. She is not an easy woman, but as her keeper, I will help her heal."

"Well…if that's your plan, you have a long road ahead of you."

Arik nodded. "This is true."

"I wish you luck. On that note, Serra and I are going to take that break," Archer said as he stood up.

"Yeah, yeah," Cal muttered as he continued to play the game with Takeshi. "Take your break, but I don't want to hear about it."

Archer waited to speak until he was alone with Serra in the corridor outside of the conference room. "I want you to promise me something."

She looked up at him solemnly. "All right."

"Promise me that we are never going to travel with your fathers ever again."

She giggled, then let out a protest when he began pulling her down the hallway. "This isn't the way to our room."

"How observant of you. We aren't going to our room. We're going to spend a little time in here." Archer pulled her to a stop in front of the holo room. He pressed a button on the control panel. "Begin Archer, relaxation program alpha one."

"*Program is activated and running.*"

The door to the holo room slid opened and they stepped out onto a balcony overlooking a mountain vista with a backdrop of stars shimmering over a midnight sky. A large hot tub was set into the center of the balcony, surrounded by hundreds of candles. Steam rose from the hot water in contrast to the cool night air.

Serra breathed in the sultry fragrance of night jasmine, then turned to smile at him. "This is absolutely perfect."

"I'm glad you think so. One day I would like to take you somewhere like this for real. Until then, the holo room can take us anywhere we want to go. Come on, hummingbird. Let's get in."

They undressed in companionable silence, then sunk into the steaming water with matching groans of delight. "This is perfect," she repeated on a long sigh.

"Almost...there we are. Now it's perfect," Archer said after pulling her into his arms so she relaxed against him.

"I know you and Jax hate being cooped up on a cruiser, but I don't mind them anymore. I guess I'm just used to it after all the traveling I've done."

"You know, this wouldn't be a bad way to spend my time. I thought about just giving up my position to travel with you full time. Sort of like what Jack did when he and Ian claimed Donna. But that wouldn't be fair to Jax."

Serra understood completely. "I would never ask for either of you to do that for me."

"You wouldn't, but I don't like the idea of spending long amounts of time away from you."

"I know."

"But this is nice. There are so many places I want to go with you. So many experiences I want to share. I always find it sort of strange using the holo rooms. It feels real, even though I know it's not."

"I could explain holo tech to you in detail, but I think I'd rather do something else right now..."

Serra turned in his arms, catching his lips with her as she ran her hands up his hard, muscular chest. She loved the feeling of his bare skin, and moved her hand between them, lower until she gripped his erection in the water.

"You're supposed to be relaxing," he growled.

"We can relax...after," she whispered, nipping at his lower lip.

His lips crushed down on hers, voraciously feeding off of her as she met him beat for beat. The heat of lust burned bright as her body trembled against his. She sucked on his tongue as he shoved it into her mouth, driving them both crazy with need.

Her arms wrapped around his neck as he shifted her, rubbing his hard cock against her slick pussy. Jerking her tighter against him, he ground their bodies together. He let out a growl of need, and his large hands gripped her ass as she began rocking her hips against him.

It wasn't enough.

She needed more…so much more.

Reaching between them, she grabbed hold of his thick cock, stroking the hard shaft with her hand. He groaned when she swirled her thumb over the head of his cock, teasing them both.

"Two can play that game."

In response, she gasped in pleasure as two of his fingers shoved inside her tight hole. "Oh, God! Sully!"

"Do you like that, baby? Do you think that feels as good as your hand wrapped around my cock?"

"Yes," she moaned, beyond speech now as he thrust inside her. She whimpered as he curled those clever fingers so they hit her G-spot, his thumb rubbing gently over her clit. She began moving her hand up and down his thick cock again as their mouths met in another scorching kiss.

"It's not enough. Put me inside you, hummingbird. Do it before I lose my mind."

Holding onto his shaft, she slowly lowered herself onto him. She let out a moan as her head fell back when she was full of his cock. It felt so good, like he was a part of her. Every time he touched her, it was like he was touching her soul.

She starting rocking on him, slowly, feeding the flames of desire between them. She loved when he touched her so tenderly, but there were times—like now—when she wanted to be taken. To be conquered.

When she wanted him to own her.

On her next stroke she paused when she was seated to the hilt. Feeling a little wicked, she smiled. "Perhaps I should just sit here a while. You did say you wanted to relax…right?"

"God damn it, Serra. Don't fuck with me now. I'm riding the edge."

She leaned forward so her breath brushed over his lips. "I'd rather you ride me."

Gasping, she found herself lifted off of him and spun around so she faced the edge of the hot tub. Her hands braced against the wooden slates of the balcony floor as she was bent over. She moaned as he ran his hands over her ass, kneading the smooth flesh, then let out a startled yelp as his hand came down on her ass in a hard slap.

"Tease me, will you? Spread your legs for me. Wider!" He barked out the harsh command. "You want me to ride you? Get ready because you're gonna get exactly what you asked for."

She spread her legs further and arched her back a second before he gripped her hips hard and shoved his entire cock into her with one hard thrust. She let out a wild scream as he began fucking her with long, deep strokes.

"Fuck, your pussy feels so damn good. So fucking tight!"

"Fuck me, Sully. Give it to me."

"You'll get what I give you. All of me, Serra. You have all of me. Can you handle that?" he growled out.

"Everything. You're everything to me. I love you so much, Sully."

He pressed his body over her back, pushing her until she was flat against the balcony as he powered into her. His hands reached up, linking with hers. "I love you, Serra" he whispered in her ear. "This is me loving you, baby."

Archer pounded into her with a fast, punishing rhythm. His thick shaft was squeezed tight each time he pushed back into her. The pleasure was so acute, he could barely breathe, but he couldn't stop. Wouldn't stop pushing them toward the ecstasy that awaited them both.

The sound of their flesh slapping and of the water churning around them was an erotic symphony. He gave into the desperate pleasure as she began pushing back on him, driving him further inside of her each time he thrust. Knowing that he couldn't hold back much longer, he reached between them, rubbing at her clit with the pads of two of his fingers.

"Look at me, Serra," Archer bit out. He released one of her hands, yanked at her hair back to turn her head so she was looking at him again. "Eyes on me, baby. I need to see you come. I want to see the pleasure take you."

Bright green eyes met his and he fused his mouth to hers, capturing her scream when she shattered. She went wild, bucking beneath him, clenching down so tight on him that he couldn't move. He let out a feral snarl as he followed her over. Hips jerking as he spilled himself inside her. He buried face into the crook of her neck as he whispered his love for her one last time.

They lay there for long moments, trying to catch their breath. "Was that on your infamous list, my little hummingbird?"

She wheezed out a laugh. "No, but it should have been."

Archer jerked at the sound of the door to the holo room sliding open, then relaxed again as he saw Jax enter. Frowning at them, Jax braced his hands on his hips.

"Well, hell. You started without me."

"You snooze, you lose, bro," Archer said, nuzzling Serra's throat. "You snooze, you lose."

"The schematics were just transferred. Takeshi said we should have a location soon."

"That's good news." Serra glanced up, and a slow grin curved her lips as Jax began to undress. "Perhaps we should celebrate."

"Just what I had in mind…"

Chapter Thirteen

New Vega was a floating pleasure palace in space.

On approach, it looked like a large destroyer-class vessel, made of a black metal and dark tinted glass that blended seamlessly into the backdrop of space. The owners of New Vega took the safety of their patrons seriously. No expense had been spared to outfit the ship with defenses, as well as power weapons, making it an almost impenetrable fortress.

But inside, it was a whole different world.

The cruiser docked in one of the landing bays and half of their party left to enter New Vega by a separate entrance that had been arranged with the Krytos owners so anyone watching wouldn't see them arriving together. Serra, Jax and Archer walked toward the main doors with Skylar, Officers Ryans, Meyer and Rhine following behind them. The large doors leading into New Vega slide open silently, and a barrage of sounds assailed them all at once.

The stark gray of the landing bay gave way to the cream and gold opulent interior of New Vega. Laughter and music drifted through the perfumed air, and Serra paused as two beautiful women with breasts the size of large melons came forward to greet the men.

She had never really given the women who worked on New Vega much thought, but that changed as she saw the double take her men did at seeing the female greeters ample assets on display through their transparent gold sarong dresses. She frowned as the two women practically rubbed up against Jax and Sully as they placed leis of white flowers around their necks. Serra shared a look with Skylar as her friend moved to her side.

"Oh, hell no," Skylar muttered under her breath. "No wonder men like to come here so often. Are those things even real?"

"I don't believe that's anatomically possible."

Skylar let out a snicker. "Want me to drop those bitches for you?"

Serra considered her friend's offer for the briefest of moments before shaking her head. "Not worth it."

"I disagree, but it's your call," Skylar groused, then lowered her voice into a purr. "Well, well. Now we're talking…"

Serra turned her head in the direction Skylar was looking and blinked in surprise as two enormous men walked up to them holding leis made of pale pink flowers. The male greeters had skin tanned a dark, golden-brown, and their bare chests were oiled to a gleaming shine. Both males wore a sarong wrap around their waists, but the cloth was short enough to reveal their muscular thighs.

One of the men stepped forward to place his lei around Skylar's neck, using it to pull her closer. A sharp bang sounded from above, and Serra looked up to see Dominic and Arik up on one of the balconies, glaring down at Skylar. Serra was about to warn her, but was distracted as the other male greeter moved forward. Before he could touch her, Jax ripped the lei out of the male greeter's hand and growled, "I don't fucking think so."

The lei was unceremoniously shoved over Serra's head, then Jax pulled her away from the other males. "Hypocrite," Serra accused softly, but gentled her rebuke with a small smile.

Jax glowered at her. "I'd rather not start our vacation off by killing someone."

"At least you didn't break the building." Serra looked up just in time to watch Dom toss away a broken piece of the railing.

Archer leaned in so his lips were close to her ear. "I wasn't really looking…I was just trying to figure out how those women were able to stand up straight with those implants. You'd think they'd fall over or something."

"Stop wondering," Serra said dryly.

She shot him a glare as he coughed to cover up his laughter, then yelped as Jax pulled her roughly into his arms. "You know damn well we aren't interested in anyone but you."

176

"I know," she said with a happy sigh, but lost her smile when one of the female greeters spoke.

"I would be pleased to show you to your room."

No way in hell.

"That's okay," Serra said with an icy smile as the woman moved toward Archer again. "I believe we can find our own way."

"Fierce," Jax breathed out before nipping her ear with his teeth.

"I'll show you fierce. If she comes anywhere near our room, I'm asking that mountain over there to carry my bags," Serra whispered back tilting her head toward one of the large male greeters who patiently waited a few steps away.

Jax's eyes narrowed. "Not going to happen."

He picked up her bag himself, then gestured their entourage forward. They had only walked a few steps when Tania Lysander-Dobbs stormed up in front of them and slapped Serra hard across the face.

"You stupid whore! You've ruined everything!"

Hearing his woman cry out had Jax's blood boiling, and he had to force himself not to strike back against the older woman. Instead, he pushed Serra into Archer's arms and stepped in front of them, meeting Tania's furious gaze with his own.

"If you ever strike my chosen again, I will break your fucking hand."

Tania must have recognized the icy blast of his barely controlled rage in those softly spoken words, because she stumbled back a step, straight into Skylar's waiting arms. She let out a screech of protest as Skylar roughly jerked her hands behind her back.

"Give me a reason, you bitch," Skylar whispered gleefully as she slapped on the restraints. "Please resist and give me a reason to knock your stupid ass unconscious."

"What is the meaning of this? Unhand me!"

Holding a hand to her cheek, Serra tried to move to Jax's side, but he used an arm to hold her behind him. "No, baby. You stay away from her."

Serra sighed. "Well, at least she made it easy to find her."

"She did," Jax agreed, then turned his attention back to the struggling woman when she let out a wild screech of pain.

Skylar shot him an innocent look as she held up one of her bare hands, so only their group could see the energy crackling along her palm like faint wisps of blue lightning. "It was only a little jolt. She'll live."

Jax ignored her, focusing all his wrath on the woman who had terrorized his beloved as a child, and cost them years of happiness together. His smile was downright feral as he said, "I've been looking forward to speaking with you, Tania. In fact, I'd say I've been waiting years for it."

Dark satisfaction filled him as the woman went still, and all the color drained from her face. "I don't have anything to say to you. Serra, you tell them to let me go! How can you let them treat your mother like this?"

"You stopped being my mother the second you messed with my mind," Serra said, her voice devoid of all emotion. Tania's mouth dropped open and her eyes widened in fear.

"Take her up to our suite," Archer ordered Skylar and the officers after he noticed the attention they were getting from the crowd. As they left, he gently lifted a hand to touch the red mark on Serra's cheek, and couldn't stop his own hands from shaking with anger. "Are you all right, baby?"

"I'm fine. Or I will be. Let's just get this done."

Archer watched Serra carefully as she huddled in front of her data unit with Takeshi.

He had to admire how well she was taking the entire situation, but he was also worried. She was excellent at compartmentalizing, and was focused on finishing their mission before she dealt with her emotions. It might not be the healthiest of reactions, but it was how she processed bad situations and kept working. God knew she'd had enough of those in her life so she'd had plenty of practice. He knew there would be fallout later, but he would be there for her when that happened.

Both he and Jax would always be there for her.

Hell, Archer had to keep it together, especially after Jax had all but lost his shit. The worst of Jax's rage had been alleviated by slamming his fist through the wall as soon as they had entered the privacy of their suite. Archer was used to Jax's tantrums, but they had both been worried about Serra's reaction. Even at his worst, Archer knew that Jax would never hurt her, but she might not understand Jax's need to release some of his aggression in a physical way.

But after Jax hit the wall, Serra had simply raised a brow and frowned at him. "You're going to pay for that...and apologize to the owners."

Stars, Archer loved her.

They had secured Tania Lysander-Dobbs in the conference room located within their suite. It was equipped with soundproofing and high-grade locks, which made it the perfect temporary holding cell for their prisoner. They'd decided to leave her in the room while they waited for the rest of their team to arrive, then they'd argued about who would get to interrogate her.

It didn't help that everyone wanted a shot at Tania.

In the end, it was decided that Jax, Dom and High Commander Newgate would take the first run at questioning her. Archer had wanted to go in with them, but he'd needed to hold Serra while she had watched more then he'd needed to assuage his own anger.

It enraged him when he'd felt her shaking as Tania had confessed to bribing her way on to Tartarus, where she had brokered the deal to have Serra programmed with the *xili* drug back when she was seventeen. And for what? Pure and simple greed. Tania had known Serra was the key to ensuring she had been able to live the lifestyle she had always wanted, and she'd been enraged when she'd heard about Serra's claiming ceremony through her network of gossip.

Tania has sneered at Jax when she had answered. "I saw the way you looked at her. I had to do something. You would have ruined everything if you had claimed Serra when she turned eighteen, and I couldn't allow that. You still managed to get your way, even though I paid good credits to make sure she stayed away from you."

As she had been questioned, she didn't hold anything back. Now that she had been caught there was no need. It was apparent that she didn't understand how much trouble she was in, but it wasn't their duty to inform her of the ramifications of what she'd done until they were finished.

Halfway through the interrogation, Serra had turned around and walked over to the living room to open her data unit. "I've seen enough. She's nothing to me now."

Takeshi also turned his back on the viewing screen, and after sharing a look with Archer, moved to sit down next to Serra on the couch to help her with her work. Archer shifted in his position so he could continue to watch the interrogation, and still keep his eye on his chosen. He was sickened by the way Tania continued to speak about how she had betrayed her own daughter with such ease, answering whatever questions she was asked. It wasn't until Jax demanded to know about the theft of Serra's work that Archer caught her lie.

"I'm telling you, I don't know what you're talking about. Who cares about that stuff, anyways. Serra just hands it all over to the Alliance, so why are you asking me?"

"Where is your assistant Eloise?" Dom pressed.

180

Tania's lips tightened in distain before she spat out, "Why the hell do I care? I fired that useless girl a week ago."

The men called a break and left Tania in the conference room, but when she saw Cade and Andrew standing in the doorway, she began to scream, demanding to be set free. "Do something! Help me, you fools!"

Ignoring her, Cade closed the door to the conference room himself, locking her in. "I always knew there was something wrong with her," Cade began. "But I never knew she was just plain evil."

Andrew turned to High Commander Newgate. "Sir, I'd like to officially request that our claim on Tania be stricken from—"

"Already done," Roman Newgate said. "Your bond was broken the moment she committed treason by conspiring with the Tarins and used *xili* on your daughter."

"She's hiding something, but I need a break away from that bloody bitch," Jax muttered as he stalked over to stand behind Serra. Needing to do something for her, he began to rub her shoulders.

"So do I," Dom said as he rolled his neck to relieve the tension there. "Stars, she deserves the worst mother of the fucking century award." He winced as he turned in Serra's direction to apologize.

"Don't worry. I agree with you," she assured him.

"Archer and I will take the next round," Arik said. "She was lying about her assistant."

"She was," Archer agreed.

Jax leaned over and pressed a kiss onto the top of Serra's head. "Come on, sweetheart. Why don't we take a little break—"

Serra tilted her head up. "We could...or I could tell you that the Strike Force Team you sent out got the buyer."

"No shit?"

She nodded then let out a laugh when Jax lifted her straight up off the couch, turning her to press a hard kiss on her mouth.

"The buyers were tracked to a small outpost outside the Odalla sector on Reema," Takeshi said as he fingers blurred over the keyboard. The viewing screen on the wall switched from showing Tania sitting in the conference room to the footage taken from a camera that had been on one of the Strike Force team members during the takedown. "The team found a group of marauders that have been known for trading in black market goods."

"Any survivors?" Roman Newgate asked.

"Two. Five were killed in the takedown. No casualties for the Strike Force."

"I need coffee." Serra turned away from the violence on screen, trying to hold back a yawn.

"I'll get it." Officer Ryans popped up from his seat and hurried over to the food console.

"I want Officers Nolan and Prentice taken into custody. They're here on New Vega, and I want them in interrogation. Since Eloise Greer is in the wind, they might know where she is."

Officers Meyer and Rhine stood up from where they had been sitting. "Sir, we can go now," Officer Rhine offered. "I know where Nolan usually likes to gamble."

"We'll go with you," Cade said. "I need to get out of this suite for a bit. Just knowing Tania is in the other room is..."

"Making me sick," Andrew finished. He walked over kiss Serra's cheek. "We'll be back soon."

The four men left the suite while the others continued watching the video of the takedown on Reema. Serra smiled gratefully at Officer Ryans as he handed her a steaming mug of coffee, giving Skylar the other mug he was holding. He walked around the room, distributing the other mugs, then went to stand next to Jax as they watched the screen.

"The Strike Force team is damn good," Jax commented.

"Commander Malloy's group is one of the best," High Commander Newgate said with no small amount of pride.

"You work with them a lot, don't you?" Archer asked.

"I do. I've spent quite a bit of time with them since my position requires me to do a lot of traveling."

182

Skylar's eyes were alight with interest and a hint of envy. "Do they have any female members on the Strike Force teams?"

Dom shot her a dark glare from across the room. "No."

Roman Newgate started to respond, but the sound of Arik crashing to the floor had everyone moving. "What the hell happened?"

Archer blinked to clear his vision, only it didn't help. He took a step forward then dropped the mug of coffee he was holding as he fell to the floor when he limbs went numb. Seeing Serra on the ground in front of him, he tried to crawl toward her. Fear swept through him as she turned her head to stare at him through glassy eyes. He was barely aware of the others falling. The only thing that mattered was getting to Serra.

He reached out his hand, fingertips brushing hers as he whispered her name, then lost his fight to stay conscious as the darkness claimed him.

Jax let out a groan as he prayed for the pounding in his head to dissipate.

It had been years since he had last been on a bender and woken up with such a headache. No, that wasn't right. He hadn't been drinking. He had been watching a video when—his thoughts cleared even as his head continued to pound like it was going to explode.

Jerking up, Jax surveyed the room as he fought back the urge to puke his guts out. They were on New Vega in their suite, and everyone in the room was passed out where they had dropped to the ground. Pain tore through his heart when he saw that Serra and Skylar were both missing.

Serra!

His body felt heavy, but he pushed himself forward, crawling over to Dom where he lay a few feet away. Jax reached out, checking for his friends pulse, and let out a relieved sigh when he found it beating strong. Without hesitation, Jax lifted his hand and slapped Dom across the face, then lifted his arm barely in time to block the fist that flew at his face in retaliation.

"What the fuck?"

"We've been drugged."

"Serra!"

He turned and met Archer's desolate eyes, and Jax let the ice cold rage build inside of him. She was still alive. Whoever did this wouldn't have taken her just to kill her. They would get her back. There was no option for failure.

"Son of a—Dom! Arik's pulse is thready and he's not waking up!" Roman Newgate was bent over Arik, trying to wake the D'Aire to no avail.

"Fuck...the D'Aire react differently than we do to certain drugs," Dom said as he crawled over to his friend when his legs failed to allow him to stand. He lifted his wrist to call for a med tech, but turned his head at the urgency in Archer's voice.

"Jax! I need you over here!"

Jax made it to his knees before he had to reach out and to hold onto the couch to steady himself when his legs remained numb. He let out a roar of rage as he saw Archer braced over Cal Ryans, holding his shirt to a chest wound that was bleeding out fast.

"I didn't drink...the...coffee," Ryans panted out. "They...took...the women...I couldn't stop them."

Jax stumbled over to them and surveyed the damage for himself. A hilt of a knife was sticking out of Ryans' chest, and the younger man had lost a lot of blood while the rest of them had been passed out. "Hold on, kid. You hold the hell on!"

"Called...for help...sorry, sirs."

"You have nothing to be sorry about. Don't you fucking die on me, Ryans. That's a goddamn order!"

Even as he spoke, the door to the suite burst open as a dozen men rushed in, led by Serra's fathers. "Christ, what the fuck happened here?"

Two med techs hurried over and went to work on Cal's injury. "Missed the heart, but we need to stop the bleeding…"

Jax struggled to his feet, stepping back to give the men room to try and save the young officer. He looked down at the blood on his hands. His friend's blood. The sounds in the room became muffled until the beat of his heart was the only thing he heard.

The heart that belonged to Serra.

Someone had taken his woman, and there would be a reckoning the likes no one had ever seen if she was hurt…or worse. He'd failed to protect Serra, but he would get her back.

At any cost.

"Where is my daughter, Jax?" Andrew shouted, but Jax just ignored him as he moved toward the door to the conference room. It took him two tries to unlock the door since his hands were covered with blood. When the door opened, he saw horror in Tania's eyes as she got a good look at him. Jumping up from her chair, she backed away.

"Don't touch me! Help!"

Jax didn't stop advancing until he gripped her by the throat. Ruthlessly, he slammed her back against the wall, lifting her off her feet. "Where is she?"

Archer, Cade and Andrew rushed in. "Jax! What are you doing, man?"

"She knows something!" Jax roared back, not taking his gaze off the petrified woman in his grasp. His mind was a red haze of fury, and he wanted retribution so bad he could almost taste it.

"I don't know anything!" Tania gasped.

"Liar!" Jax snarled, letting her see that he was no longer the calm man who had questioned her before.

"Jax, we can track Serra. We'll get her back."

"Then do it," Jax snapped back at Archer. "But this bitch is going to tell me what she knows, if I have to take her apart, piece by piece. You wouldn't just fire your assistant. She knows too many of your secrets for you to just let her go. And you're going to tell me everything, because if Serra dies, so will you. Do you hear me? Your life depends on if I get her back. So, start talking."

Eye wide with terror, Tania spilled out everything she knew.

Chapter Fourteen

Serra held back a groan of pain as she came to lying on the cold, hard floor.

She stayed very still as she did an internal survey, and realized that she was undamaged by whatever had happened. After years of getting those raging headaches every time she thought of Jax and Archer, the throbbing in her head barely fazed her. She started to shift her body, but the sound of a metallic thud had her freezing in place.

"You are awake, human?"

Turning her head, Serra opened her eyes to see a pair of cat-like, amber eyes staring back at her. Jumping to a wobbly crouch, Serra braced herself for an attack.

But none came.

A single Helios female stood staring back at her curiously, head cocking to the side with feline grace. The Helios were from the planet Helix, a jungle world that was almost primitive in nature. Known as shifters for their ability to change into large jungle cats, the Helios were some of the most dangerous beings in the known worlds.

"You have nothing to fear from me."

Nodding, Serra studied the beautiful female as she rose to her feet, swaying for a moment before she got her bearings. The Helios had golden skin with long hair a few shades lighter. She was dressed in tight brown leather pants and a matching vest that showed off her generous curves and corded muscles. Combined with her slanted amber eyes and standing at a few inches over six feet tall, she was an impressive sight.

Serra noticed a camera on the ground by the female's feet. Glancing back up, Serra could see the wires sticking out of the wall where the camera used to be attached in the corner of the cell.

When she met the Helios' gaze again, there was satisfaction gleaming in those cat eyes.

"I was angry when I woke, and I don't like being monitored."

"I don't blame you."

Serra took a quick survey and saw they were in some sort of holding cell with an electrical field holding them in. On the floor next to her was Skylar, who was still lying in an unconscious heap. "Do you know where we are? And how is it you have a language converter? I thought most Helios don't like getting the implant."

"We're on some sort of vessel. We were taken from New Vega, but I just woke before you, so I don't know much more. I am Reva, warrior of the Golaris tribe, and guard to Ambassador Golaris and her companions. Since we travel off planet, all guards are required to have the implant."

Serra eyes widened. "Solange Golaris? She is Ambassador Golaris now? A few years ago, I met her and the companions she has life-locked with when I was on Helix, back she was leader of your tribe. My name is Serra Lysander...well, it's Serra Spartan-Archer now."

"Protector Serra, the ambassador spoke very highly of you when you came to upgrade the shield over our world. Ambassador Golaris is my mother. During your visit I was away on The Hunt, or I would have met you then."

The Hunt was a rite of passage for all Helios when they turned twenty. They were left out in the jungle for a week and had to survive on their own in the harsh terrain. Because the Helios were a matriarchal society, both females and males were put through the same test...and many never made it back.

Only the strong survived.

If Reva had survived The Hunt, then she'd returned to her tribe as a proven warrior, and would have received a thin scar across her heart as a badge of honor.

"Our captors are humans," Reva said. "I was doing a security sweep of the docking bays with another of my tribe before my mother arrived when I witnessed two humans being slain. I went to help, but my partner and I were stunned from behind. I woke up here shortly after with the two of you. From the vibrations, I could tell we'd already left New Vega."

They both looked over as Skylar let out a groan, then she bolted into a sitting position with her fists clenched in front of her. Seeing Serra and Reva, Skylar lay back down and flung her arm over her eyes. "What the hell happened?"

Serra filled her in, and Skylar lowered her arm to glance at Reva as the Helios spoke. "I am glad neither of you are crying. Human females always seem to cry. It is annoying."

"We aren't the crying type," Skylar said dryly as she sat up, bracing her elbows on her raised knees. Skylar hated feeling out of control. Someone would pay for drugging them, she thought darkly. She was damn glad that both she and Serra were wearing the comfortable pants and shirts they had been wearing when they were taken, telling her that they hadn't been messed with while they'd be unconscious. Rolling to her feet, Skylar hissed at the ache in her hip that told her she'd been dropped on it when they had been tossed in the prison cell.

Someone would definitely pay for that as well…

The three women looked over as the outer doors in the cargo bay slid open, and Eloise Greer entered the room with two men. The men had on dirty clothes, with blasters strapped to their sides and what looked like homemade knives sticking out of their dirty boots. Both of the men sneered and Serra felt sickened by the lust in their gazes.

"Well, well. Looks like everyone is up from their nap."

The usually conservative assistant looked completely different with her brown hair tumbling down around her shoulders. Dressed in a tight brown shirt that showed off her cleavage and tight beige pants, she grinned at them as she stood with her hands on her hips. "You don't know how happy I am to see you bitches in there."

"Eloise," Serra said. "Why are you doing this?"

"What part?" Eloise asked with a wild laugh. "Do you mean the part where I had you kidnapped or the part where I stole from you? You thought you were so smart. God, you damn scrolls actually believed all this time you were better than me."

"I never—"

"Shut up!" Eloise screamed. She took a moment to calm herself, then grinned again. "This really was way too easy. When you turned me down as your assistant, I was furious, until I realized that I could make more credits just stealing your work from you to sell on the black market. All I had to do was put up with your bitch of a mother. She really is a total psycho, you know."

Serra held back her snort of derision at how ironic that statement was. "I'm aware of that. So, this is all about credits?"

Eloise laughed. "Of course it is. With the added bonus of proving I'm better than you. Some genius you are. And I did it all right under your nose. I never expected Tania would make it so easy for me to get your schematics, but the old bitch actually paid me to place a block on your data unit. From there, it was easy to take what I wanted. In a way you owed me, anyways."

"How did you manage to drug us?" Skylar asked, moving to stand next to Serra and Reva.

"All I had to do was bribe one of the employees who worked in reservations to find out what suite you were in. I snuck in early and hid in one of the air vents, after I drugged the coffee. I know how much you like your coffee," she said to Serra with a conspiratorial wink. "I could have killed you all, but you're worth more to me alive. I did have to take out that young officer with my knife, but he shouldn't have tried to stop me. Once everyone was out, all I had to do was open the door for my associates, and we carted you right out in cargo containers."

"Easy peasy," one of the men said lazily as he eyed Skylar.

"You plan to sell us," Reva said flatly.

"Well, isn't the little kitty smart. Yes, I'm going to sell you. There are many Tarin who will pay big credits for human women,

190

and even more for a shifter. You I didn't expect, but you saw my men kill Charles and Jacob, so we had to take you."

"You killed Officers Nolan and Prentice?" Serra felt her heart stutter as Eloise talked about killing someone with such vicious calm. It tore her to pieces inside to know that this crazy woman had killed Officer Ryans back in the suite, but to kill two other men that she had spent time with?

Eloise stared back at her with a mad gleam in her eyes that almost looked like pleasure. "They were fun while it lasted. It was easy to recruit them to work for me, but they had outlived their usefulness. Now, it will be a while before we get close to Tartarus where we're meeting my contact. You might as well get some sleep, since I doubt you will get much once you're sold."

"I'm going to enjoy gutting you and bathing in your blood," Reva growled in a low animalistic rumble. Her eyes burned bright as she fought back the change, denying herself the shift into her cat form.

"That's…graphic," Skylar muttered. "But I think I might enjoy watching that. This crazy cunt needs killing."

"Don't you talk to me that way!" Eloise screeched out. "You can't get out. There is an electrical field holding you in that cage that will fry you if you touch it."

"Hey El, can't we have a taste of them now?" the other man asked.

"These three are too valuable." Eloise smiled at the women. "They killed the last woman I let them have. So, remember. Even if you did manage to get out, I have seven men working for me on this ship, all who are fully armed. Behave, or I just might let them have you."

She turned to leave then stopped to look back at Serra. "Oh, and if you're hoping for your big, bad, bonded to save you, think again. This vessel is now armed with the stealth tech you so graciously provided me with. We installed it yesterday. I win."

"Later, kitty." One of the men blew Reva a kiss, then chuckled as she bared her sharp teeth at him. Eloise laughed as the cocky bitch left the room with two men trailing behind her.

There was a beat of silence, then Skylar turned to Serra. "That fuckhead is not selling us. What's your plan to get us out of here?"

"You heard the woman," Reva said, looking at Skylar like she wasn't too bright. "We cannot get past the electrical field."

Skylar pointed at Serra. "Serra here is one of the smartest people in the universe, if not the smartest. She'll think of a plan...she always has a plan."

"Give me a minute. I'm thinking."

"See? She's thinking." Skylar turned to look at the transparent field that held them in the cage while she gave Serra time to come up with something. Taking a credit out of her pocket, she tossed it at the center of the invisible barrier, and watched as the coin bounce off with a crackling sound. It fell to the ground, smoking from the contact. "Well, shit."

Skylar frowned as she studied the transparent wall again. Holding up her hands a few inches away from the barrier, she tried to draw the electricity to her. Small blue streams of energy lifted from the barrier to dance along Skylar's skin. Not enough to shut it down, but it gave her enough of a jolt to kill the last of the lethargy cause by the drug. Frustrated, she turned away and saw Reva staring at her with wide eyes.

"I'm a conduit," Skylar explained holding her hands up again, showing the shifter the streams of energy racing over her skin. "I can manipulate energy, but it works better on people than shit like this."

"Fascinating."

"I think I have something." Serra said. "I need to get to the control panel on the other side of the cell wall. If we can access it from here, I can override the system and shut it down. I'll need you to give me a few minutes to get to that data center so I can lock them out. We're in a cargo bay of some kind, and I don't like thinking they could just open the doors and suck us out into space."

"Yeah, that would definitely suck. Reva and I can give you the time you need, but what the hell do we do after? We won't be able to hold them off forever. Do we try for an escape pod?"

Serra's fingers drummed against her thighs as she thought about the probabilities. She was terrified and knew their circumstances were dire, but she had to focus. Their lives were depending on her...on all of them working together. Serra knew without a doubt Jax and Archer were already coming for her. She just had to make sure she gave them time to find her. "No, we have the best chance of survival if we stay here and fortify our position until help comes."

"But we have no clue when that will be," Reva pointed out.

Serra shook her head. "Considering that we were served the coffee first, I believe it's safe to assume that we consumed more of the drug and since our body masses are less than the men, they would have woken before we did, giving them more time to follow us."

Skylar and Reva looked at each other, then Skylar said, "That's great and all, but that still doesn't help them find us."

"Oh, but this will." Serra smiled as she pulled out the necklace from under the collar of her shirt. "There is a tracker in here. We just have to hold out until they find us."

A slow smile spread over Skylar's face. "That's pretty damn handy, even though it's kind of creepy your bonded have you tagged. So, we need to break through the wall?"

"Yes. About right here," Serra said placing her hand on the wall. "I noticed Eloise looking in this area as if making sure we were locked in. I'm guessing this is where the control panel is, but I could be wrong."

"I trust you," Skylar said, then frowned at Reva as she handed her the destroyed camera. "What? You want me to break through the wall with this?"

"No, I want you to give me a noisy distraction."

Understanding lit up Skylar's eyes, and she quickly moved over to the other side of the cage, away from Serra and Reva. Skylar stood at the ready with the broken camera in her hand. She gave a nod to Reva, who turned her hand into a claw and punched it through the wall at the same time Skylar threw the camera into the electric field. The camera snapped and sizzled before it fell to the ground in burnt pile of metal, creating enough noise to cover up what Reva was doing.

Reva pulled her hand out and moved across the cell to stand with Skylar as Serra reached into the opening in the wall so she was able to access the wires. The door to the cargo bay slid open and the two men rushed inside, brandishing their blasters.

"What the hell was that? You stupid cunts, are you trying to get yourselves fried?"

The men grinned at each other while they put away their weapons when Reva turned her back to them and took off her vest. "What are you doing?" Skylar hissed.

"I don't want to ruin my clothes," Reva replied softly as she began to unfasten her pants.

The men took another step toward the prison cell. "Damn, this bitch is hot for it. I say to hell with what Eloise says, I want to fuck one of them."

"Hey, where's the other one?"

Serra did her best to ignore the men as she hurried to reconnect the wires inside the wall. She saw the shimmering electrical field dissipate, leaving the entrance to their prison cell open, then let out a curse as the lights went out and an alarm started to sound. One of the men looked over and saw her just as the overhead emergency lights kicked on. The guard's eyes widened as he reached for his blaster.

"Now!" Serra yelled.

Skylar rushed the man, reaching out to grip the arm holding the weapon as she wrapped her other hand around his neck. His body

194

went rigid and he stared at her in horror as she ruthlessly drew his energy from him. At the same time, Reva spun around and shifted in one seamless motion, hitting the other man full force as a large, sleek jungle cat. She cut off the sound of his scream as the cat bit down on his neck, taking him down to the floor.

As soon as they were freed, Serra raced across the room and started hacking into the ship's onboard system through the data console. Images of Eloise blasting them out into space had Serra pushing hard to lockdown the outer doors so they couldn't be killed that way. Next, she cut off the controls to the cargo bay doors leading to the rest of the ship so the rest of the kidnappers couldn't attack them.

It wouldn't hold forever, but it would give them some time.

She tried to shut off the alarm, but couldn't access that system from the cargo bay. Serra turned as she heard Skylar mutter something from behind her and froze in shock as she saw the two men sprawled out on the floor. One of the men's eyes were wide with horror as he lay dead on the ground, while the other was a bloody, mangled mess. Reva in cat-form snarled and swiped at the dead body with her massive paw again. The cat was huge, and reminded Serra of the pictures she'd once seen of the ancient saber tooth tigers that had once roamed Earth. She felt a jolt of unease at the Helios turned its head and bared its long fangs in a triumphant growl.

"Okay, I never realized how fucking big those cats are," Skylar whispered as she inched her way around Reva.

"They can crush a skull with one bite," Serra said, making Skylar frown at her as she moved to her side.

"Thanks," Skylar said dryly. "I really didn't need to know that now that we're stuck in here with it." They turned as pounding sounded on the doors leading to the interior of the ship. Reva let out a vicious snarl towards the door as they heard men yelling. "We need weapons."

Reva suddenly shifted back into her naked humanoid form, and held up a hand to stop Serra and Skylar from moving. "I hear fighting in the corridor outside."

"I can't hear shit over these alarms."

"Shifters have very good hearing. You have a very impressive power," she said to Skylar.

Skylar let out a little laugh. "I'd have to say turning into an eight hundred pound cat with claws as big as my fucking arm is more impressive."

Reva's smile froze then she let out a growl. "The men are breaking through. Stay behind me." She shifted back to her cat-form and backed up so she was guarding Skylar and Serra.

The doors opened an inch and Serra heard Jax's voice boom out her name.

"Jax! We're in here!"

The men in the hallway pried open the heavy doors, and elite soldiers poured into the room, weapons at the ready. Serra let the tears come now as she ran to Jax, who tore off his helmet and dropped his weapon. He caught her up against him so tight she could barely breathe. The hard armor of his black uniform pressed against her painfully, but she didn't care.

"Serra! Oh, God…I thought…"

She could feel him shaking against her and lifted her head to press kisses over his beloved face. He claimed her lips in a heated kiss, then she found herself yanked into Archer's arms. He buried his face into her neck, whispering her name over and over in a tortured voice.

"You came for me," she whispered softly.

"Always. We'll always come for you."

She sank into his kiss, feeling Jax move up behind her so she was surrounded by them. Comfort flooded her, and the relief of knowing she was finally safe made her tremble. They stayed like that, locked together as the other soldiers surveyed the carnage inside the cargo bay.

"Sirs. We have Eloise Greer in custody."

"Good," Jax mumbled between placing kisses on Serra's neck.

"I think my friend here has a few things she wants to say to that bitch," Skylar said with a laugh. Reva let out a savage snarl that had the elites casting wary glances at the large jungle cat.

Jax wiped at the tears falling on one side of Serra's face while Sully kissed away the tears on her other cheek. "I just have one thing to ask both of you."

"What's that, sweetheart?"

She pulled back so she could look at both of her men and let out a little laugh. "What the hell took you so long?"

Epilogue

In the aftermath of their rescue, Serra thought she'd held it together pretty well.

She had pushed back her emotions, doing what needed to be done when they were back on New Vega. As they'd left that cargo bay, Serra had seen the swath of destruction that Jax and Sully had cut through to get to her. They had been ruthless as they'd boarded the kidnappers' vessel, killing everyone in their path. Instead of being afraid of what they were capable of, she was glad that she had such powerful, driven men who would do anything in order to get to her. They didn't kill indiscriminately, but they would to rescue her.

Eloise Greer was now on her way back to earth, along with Serra's mother, guarded by a dozen hard-eyed elite soldiers. Serra's fathers decided to accompany High Commander Newgate back. Cade had said he needed to see Tania locked in a cage where she would await trial with his own eyes.

Serra had been devastated when she had thought that Officer Cal Ryans had died, but he was slowly recovering from his stab wound in the medical unit. She'd demanded to stop by so she could see him, and found her assistant, Troy Takeshi, sitting next to Ryans' bed, playing a video game with him to keep the injured man entertained.

Skylar had chosen to stay on New Vega, and after her debriefing had decided to spend some time with Reva and some of the other Helios from Reva's tribe. It hadn't surprised Serra that both Dom and Arik had also chosen to stay. The sedative had acted like poison to Arik instead of just putting him to sleep, but he'd fully recovered. Dom, Arik and Skylar would be returning to Earth with Serra and her bonded, but Sully had suggested they all stay for a few more days to rest and relax.

It wasn't until they were in their new suite later that night that Serra had finally lost it. Curling up on the bed, her body had started to shake as she'd thought about everything that had happened. Jax and Sully hadn't left her side from the moment they'd stormed into the cargo bay on the kidnappers' ship. They had tracked her by using the signal in her necklace, and Sully had made her swear never to take it off again. She had made the promise, angering them again when she had thanked them for coming for her.

They would just have to get over the damn fact she had manners.

Exhausted, she'd fallen asleep surrounded by her two lovers, and was grateful when she'd dropped into a deep slumber where nightmares didn't chase her.

Now, she woke alone.

She knew that there was still a lot they had to do, but she couldn't seem to make herself move. It made her smile to see that they had left the lights on low so she wouldn't wake in the dark. A slight sound coming from the corner of the room had her jolting up to a sitting position.

"Shh, it's just me."

Archer got up from the chair in the corner and hurried over to her, pulling her into his arms. He pressed his lips to her forehead as he stroked his hand over her long, dark hair. He clutched her a little too tight, but couldn't make himself let go. There were things to be seen to, but he'd found himself back in their bedroom where he could watch over her, even in sleep. He and Jax had traded off during the long hours of the day, watching over her like sentries while the other took care of business. They had been a little concerned when she had slept through the day, but they knew she needed the rest.

"I have to…"

"Of course you do."

Archer lifted her into his arms, smiling to himself at how this scene mimicked the first time they had been together after they'd claimed her. He took her into the bathroom and left her to take care of her needs in private. Picking up the items he'd brought with him, he placed them on the bed. Seeing Serra naked had stirred his lust, but he needed to do this right. He used his wrist unit to contact Jax to let him know Serra was awake, then he took it off, setting it on the nightstand. He sat down on the bed, settling in against the headboard to wait for his love.

"How do you feel?" he asked as soon as Serra walked back into the bedroom. He smiled as she moved straight back onto the bed, curling up next to him so he could wrap his arms around her.

"I feel...afraid," she admitted softly. "But that's silly since I know I'm safe now."

"Nothing you feel is silly."

"There's our woman," Jax said as he entered the bedroom. He strode over to the bed, sitting down on the side so he could lean over to brush his lips over hers. "We thought you'd never wake up."

Archer rubbed his hand up and down her arm. "She's afraid, Jax."

They shared a look and Jax nodded. "You've been through a lot, Serra. There is nothing wrong with being afraid. It's what you do through the fear that matters. You held it together and protected yourself and the others until we could get to you. That took courage."

Serra basked in the glow of their approval, but it still didn't lessen her feelings of being slightly lost. Glancing down to the end of the bed, she frowned at a length of rope she saw laying there. "What is that?"

Archer lifted her so she was sitting up and he could look her in the eye. "There is something we want to do for you. Something we want to try."

"I don't understand," she said as she looked at both men.

"We always knew we would claim you, Serra. Over the years, both Archer and I have studied up on things we could do to help you when you had one of your episodes, or what we could do just to make you more comfortable with your surroundings."

"I know when you feel panicked you like to use your gravity cloak or a weighted blanket. We think we have something that will help you like that, only it's something we can do together. It's called *Kinbaku,* an ancient form of rope bondage." Archer paused when Serra started to protest. He placed a finger to her lips as Jax took over stroking her arms. "What we want to do isn't about control. We aren't taking anything from you. We only want to give."

"I still don't understand," she whispered. "I don't think I want to do any of that bondage stuff."

"The basic form of what we are suggesting is called *Shibari.* It's an art form, using the ropes to shape and mold a body into a sculpture, but *Kinbaku* takes it to a higher level, allowing us to use the ropes to connect with you, through our hearts, spirits and minds," Jax explained. "We don't want to hurt you. Never that. The ropes will be an extension of our hands on you, holding you tight through the binding. Are you willing to let us show you?"

Serra paused for a moment to consider what they had told her. She didn't like the thought of being restrained and out of control, and didn't see the logic of how they thought they could help her. But she was willing to try. "What if I don't like this?"

"Then we stop. Immediately," Archer said. "Neither of us have a need to use this form of control over you, Serra. Still, your gravity cloak helps you stay grounded. I think this will too, as well as being pleasurable for all of us."

She blew out a breath and nodded. "All right. I'll try it. But I want you naked, too"

"That we can do," Jax said, pressing a kiss to her naked shoulder. He and Archer undressed, feeling the heat of her eyes trailing over them as they did. When Jax sat back down on the bed, he shifted her, putting her between his own legs so she leaned back against him as she sat on the edge. Archer grabbed the rope, moving to stand in front of them.

"We are just going to create a tight corset with the rope around your chest and waist. The purpose is so you feel it wrapped around you, restraining you without really taking away any of your control. Trust us to ground you this way so you can be unbound inside."

"Each time we wrap the rope around your body I want you to think of it like it is us touching you, holding you close. Think of the ropes as an extension of our hands," Jax whispered in her ear as Archer unwound the long length of the hemp rope.

Serra held her breath as Sully looped the rope around her shoulders, over her back. She felt Jax holding it in place, and shivered as the back of his fingers brushed against her naked skin. Archer wrapped the rope around her again, making a few more loops that created a harness around her upper body, so her breasts were poking out from between the ropes.

"We are going to bind these as well," Archer said softly, pressing light kisses to each of her nipples, making them pucker. "I love how at ease you are with your body. I love looking at you."

"Then why do you want to cover them up?" she asked, trying to understand.

Kneeling in front of her, he smiled at her. "Because when we do, every time you move the ropes will brush over your skin, making you feel good."

Jax took the ends of the ropes from Archer as they wound them around her, creating loops in the back as well as the front of her body, moving lower with each pass. Archer carefully watched her face, searching for any signs of discomfort in her expression. "How are you feeling? Is it too tight?"

"No, its…I'm fine."

Archer could hear the nerves in her voice, but also the intrigue. When he had researched this discipline, he knew it would be something that they could use on her, but not as a means for taking anything away from her. Her need to be in control would prevent them from binding her arms or hands, but they didn't need or want that. That was the true gift of her submission to them.

She trusted them to give her what she needed.

Knowing that had Archer's cock hard as iron. He forced himself to continue to wrap the rope around her slowly as he fought down the raging hunger that demanded he just part her thighs and thrust into her. But he couldn't. This first session was too important, and he needed to see if this helped her before he focused on his own needs.

Serra struggled to keep still as they slowly and meticulously wound the rope around her, creating a rope corset around her torso. The sensation was pleasant, feeling the rough natural fibers of the rope against her skin, but more so, she enjoyed the pressure the ropes created as they hugged her tight. It made her feel centered, contained, in a way her gravity cloak did, but there was an added element to this.

Pleasure.

Each time Jax and Sully brushed against her, she felt her body heat. She could feel the liquid pooling between her thighs as her body readied itself for them. Closing her eyes, she focused on the feel of the rope wrapping around her in an unhurried, soothing rhythm. She imagined it was both of them hugging her close, making her feel safe within their embrace.

"I have news for you both," Jax murmured softly as he and Archer continued their work, slowly…carefully. "Roman Newgate has been offered a position on the Council of Regents. He has accepted, and informed me that I've been nominated as his replacement as High Commander."

Serra's eyes popped open and she tried to twist around to look at him. It gave her a jolt of pleasure as the rough rope rubbed against her nipples, sliding against skin. "Jax! That's wonderful!"

"If I take it, this means I'd have to travel as much as you. We would be given our own crew, and we could work out a travel schedule that would suit all our needs." Jax looked at Archer over Serra's shoulder. "I said I needed to speak to both of you before I

204

accepted. You would still be a commander, but I know this might be difficult for you."

Archer smiled at him. "If this means we can stay with Serra all the time, then I'm all for it. Who'd take over running the Capital?"

"There are a few candidates, but my first choice would be General Gabriel Titan."

"I agree," Archer said as they finished the last loop around Serra's waist. "How does that feel, hummingbird?"

"Tight, but it doesn't hurt. It feels surprisingly good," she added.

"Now, since we are all in agreement, I think we should celebrate a little," Jax murmured. "Did our chosen enjoy being wrapped up in our love?"

Archer hummed as he took in the sight of her slick pussy as he pushed her thighs open. He lifted two fingers, swirling then over her slit, lighting rubbing over her distended clit. "I would say she did."

"Do you want us to take you like this, Serra? While you are bound with the rope?" Jax demanded before sucking on the exposed skin of her neck.

"Yes, yes, I do."

Unable to wait any longer, Archer rose up to his knees and spread her thighs wider so he could settle between them and pulled her closer to the edge of the bed. He and Jax had talked it over beforehand, and the plan had been to take her together, but something about the binding ritual had touched a part of Archer's soul that he hadn't been prepared for.

He slid the head of his cock over her slick pussy, making them both groan. As if understanding Archer's need, Jax whispered in her ear. "Open for Archer, sweetheart. Feel him loving you."

Serra did as he asked, leaning back on Jax's body as Archer positioned his cock at her entrance. She felt his cock parting her tight muscles as he sank inside her and threw her head back with a moan. The rope corset hugged her body tight, making it difficult to bend and move in a way that only heightened her pleasure.

When Archer was seated to the hilt, he used the rope harness to pull her back up so he could take her mouth in a scorching kiss. Needing the connection, he stood, holding onto her, then shifted her over onto the bed so she was spread out with him over her. Jax moved to the side, stroking his own cock while he watched Archer kissing her, his body pushing her down into the mattress.

Archer couldn't stop touching her face, her hair, anywhere he could reach as he thrust inside her with more force. "Do you feel that, Serra? Do you feel us wrapped around you while I'm inside you?"

"Yes," she moaned. Serra understood now. The tight bindings around her body was like having them wrapped around her, like having Jax holding her while Archer was pressed full length over her body. She could feel the rub and burn of the rope as he moved over her, the sensations reverberating straight through her body so it pulsed in her clit.

No more words were needed as Archer began to move faster, fucking into her harder. He pulled back so he could look into her beautiful light-green eyes. Less than an inch apart, he breathed in her air, and it was something that seemed more intimate than a kiss at the moment. Archer saw the love shining back at him from her eyes, and felt like the luckiest man in the universe. He felt tied to her, in a way that he had never thought possible.

She might be the one with ropes around her, but he was the one who was bound.

To her.

Only to her.

"You are my soul, Serra. Give me your pleasure. Share it with me," Archer demanded softly, still looking into her eyes. He saw those beautiful eyes cloud, saw the pleasure take her as her body clamped tight around him. She squeezed him, her body bucking beneath him, rocking with the waves of ecstasy that coalesced between them.

206

Archer groaned as he jerked against her, filling her with his release as his semen tore from the head of his cock, making him come so hard, spots blinded his vision.

"I love you, Serra."

"Love you," she whispered breathlessly before he took her mouth again. His hips jerked as he pushed as deep as he could go, wanting to be one with her as the last few spurts of his cum filled her. He softened his kisses, touching her tenderly before he lifted off of her. He took a moment to admire her body splayed out on the bed, saw the trickle of his release spilling out of her, then moved to the side so Jax could join with her.

Jax hooked his fingers into the ropes of the harness, using it to pulled Serra's upper body into position as he knelt between her parted thighs. He slammed his hips forward, shoving his hard cock all the way inside her until he was buried deep.

Serra cried out as Jax began thrusting his cock back and forth in a hard, heavy rhythm. She felt the ropes pulling tighter around her, adding to the sensations bombarding her system and had to grip his arms to give herself an anchor as Jax slammed into her.

"Take it, take my cock inside you," Jax ordered. "Take me inside you."

Pure pleasure filled Serra at the feeling of Jax fucking his thick cock into her pussy. Another climax began to build before she had even come down from the first. With Jax holding her up by the ropes, she gave into him completely, relaxing into his embrace as he forced her body to respond to him. She began chanting his name as he began thrusting faster.

Jax grunted as he started to slam his hips harder. Needing more, he let her body fall back onto the bed, tumbling with her so his body was pressed over her. He gripped her hands with his, pulling them up over her head, staring straight into her eyes as he slid more of his cock inside her. "I can't lose this…I can never lose you, Serra. It would fucking kill me."

"I'm right here, Jax. Safe and loved."

"You are," he swore. "We love you so much. Always have, always will."

"I love you," she swore as the pleasure burned through her. "I love you both."

Jax held onto her hands with one of his as he moved the other between them, rubbing her clit as he continued to plunge into her body. He felt like a conqueror as he watched her writhing beneath him, yet he also felt like he were the one being taken. The way she gave herself to them was intoxicating. He felt the weight of the responsibility that came with that absolute trust, and cherished it. She belonged to them. Body and soul, just like they belonged to her.

"Come, sweetheart. Come and take me with you," Jax ordered as he pinched her clit.

Serra let out a scream as her body shattered. The intensity of her climax was so extreme, she began to sob. She fought, against Jax, against herself, but the jerky movements only drove her pleasure higher.

Jax lifted his hand from between them, clasping both of her hands with his so their fingers twined together. His mouth came down hard on hers, his tongue pushing deep as her body convulsed beneath him. He thrust, once, twice then let out a hoarse shout as he shot pulse after pulse of his hot, thick cream into her tight pussy.

He pressed light kisses to her lips, rubbing his hands over her as she continued to sob. Moving off of her, Jax and Archer whispered soothing love words as they quickly removed the ropes from around her body so they could rub their hands over her skin. They held her pressed tight between them, letting her come down from her sexual high in her own time.

"Are you okay, love?" Jax asked with concern.

Serra lifted her head, and with tear drenched eyes, she smiled. "I am. That was very intense. I felt like…it wasn't just a sexual release, it was like I was releasing all the pain, anger and fear inside me as well. I could because I knew you'd both be there to catch me."

"I'm glad," Archer said as he pressed his lips to her shoulder from behind. "We'll always catch you."

She closed her eyes, letting her head rest on Jax's chest as Archer pressed tighter against her back. Held tight between them, Serra realized that no matter what happened in her life they would be there with her. She'd never have to deal with anything alone ever again. With that knowledge came a comfort that soothed the ragged parts of her soul the betrayal of her mother and former friends had caused. "I love you. Always have, always will," she whispered, repeating Jax's words back to them.

"And we love you," Jax said, his deep voice rumbling out so she could feel it within his chest.

"Always," Archer vowed.

Her bonded loved her…and with that love, she could handle anything.

THE END

ABOUT THE AUTHOR

Laurie Roma lives in Chicago and mainly writes contemporary, romantic suspense, and sci-fi romance. She has always loved immersing herself in a good book and now enjoys the pleasure of creating her own. She can usually be found tapping away on her keyboard, creating worlds for her characters while she listens to music. Of course her playlist depends on her mood...but then again, so does her writing.

An avid reader of the romance genre, nothing bothers her more than annoying characters. Seriously, who wants a happy ending for someone that pisses you off? She loves tough alpha-male heroes and strong heroines that have brains as well as beauty. Her novels are filled with both passionate romance and down and dirty lust-driven interludes, as she believes both are essential to a good love story. She loves to hear from her readers and can be reached at laurieromabooks@gmail.com.

For all titles by Laurie Roma, please visit
http://laurieroma.blogspot.com

3013: THE SERIES
http://3013theseries.blogspot.com

The 3013 Series

3013: MATED by Laurie Roma
3013: RENEGADE by Susan Hayes
3013: CLAIMED by Laurie Roma
3013: STOWAWAY by Susan Hayes

15025909R00126

Printed in Great Britain
by Amazon.co.uk, Ltd.,
Marston Gate.